HEARTBREAKER

HEARTBREAKER

stories

MARYSE MEIJER

FARRAR, STRAUS AND GIROUX   NEW YORK

Meijer

Farrar, Straus and Giroux
18 West 18th Street, New York 10011

Copyright © 2016 by Maryse Meijer
All rights reserved
Printed in the United States of America
First edition, 2016

Grateful acknowledgment is made to the publications in which
these stories first appeared, in slightly different form:
580 Split ("Whole Life Ahead"), *Joyland* ("Fugue"),
Meridian ("Home"), *Portland Review* ("Heartbreaker"),
and *Reunion: The Dallas Review* ("Shop Lady").

Library of Congress Cataloging-in-Publication Data
Names: Meijer, Maryse, 1982– author.
Title: Heartbreaker : stories / Maryse Meijer.
Description: New York : FSG Originals, 2016.
Identifiers: LCCN 2015041556 | ISBN 9780374536060 (paperback) |
   ISBN 9780374714840 (e-book)
Subjects: | BISAC: FICTION / Literary. | FICTION / Short Stories (single
   author). | FICTION / Psychological.
Classification: LCC PS3613.E4264 A6 2016 | DDC 813/.6—dc23
LC record available at http://lccn.loc.gov/2015041556

Designed by Jo Anne Metsch

Our books may be purchased in bulk for promotional, educational,
or business use. Please contact your local bookseller or the
Macmillan Corporate and Premium Sales Department at
1-800-221-7945, extension 5442, or by e-mail at
MacmillanSpecialMarkets@macmillan.com.

www.fsgbooks.com • www.fsgoriginals.com
www.twitter.com/fsgbooks • www.facebook.com/fsgbooks

1   3   5   7   9   10   8   6   4   2

FOR DANIELLE

CONTENTS

HEARTBREAKER

HOME

In the truck she sits straight, her hands flat on the seat. At a stoplight, seeing that his head is turned away, she opens the door and thrusts one shoulder out into the night air before he catches her arm. He doesn't pull, just holds her still until she leans in again, slamming the door shut. When the light turns green he lets her go.

I live just down that street, she says.

Maybe on the way back I'll drop you there, he replies. She rubs her arm.

No, she says. That's all right.

———

At the restaurant she eats most of the large pizza they order, picking off the mushrooms and scooping the cheese into greasy knobs.

I need to go to the bathroom, she tells him, and he gives her a look like, *So?*

Don't eat it all while I'm gone, she says. Laminated wood squeals under her palm as she slides her hand across the table. She looks over her shoulder, to see if he is watching her. He isn't.

In the bathroom she pees half-standing over the toilet, while in the stall next to her a woman coughs.

Do you have any lipstick? the girl calls, leaning toward the woman's ankles. Please?

Sure, the woman says, and a gold tube rolls beneath her stall door.

Thank you, the girl says. At the mirror she traces her mouth bright pink, her hips jutting into the edge of the sink.

You can keep that, honey, the woman says. It's not so great on me.

When she gets back she sees him sweeping crumbs into a napkin. Despite the hard curve of his bicep his skin looks soft, a little loose, which is how she can tell he is older. Let's get some beer, she says, smiling as he looks at her mouth. He lifts his hip for his wallet, licks his finger to peel out a five.

Something light, he tells her.

At the counter a boy in a baseball cap stares at her when she orders a pitcher.

Can I see your I.D.? he asks.

She leans forward, her breasts plumping against her forearm.

No, she says.

Well, I can't just give it to you without one.

Why not?

The boy sighs. Is that guy your dad?

She shrugs. After a moment the boy turns to pull the beer from the tap.

What's your name? he asks her.

Ophelia, she lies.

Ophelia?

Yeah, she says. And I need some quarters, too.

She winks when he pours the change into her hand.

At the jukebox she punches in the numbers for a slow song. She dances by herself while men stare at her from their tables, arms curled around their paper plates. He is watching her, too, turned sideways in the booth and sucking foam from the top of his glass. She waves for him to join her and he shuffles to the broken tile of the dance floor.

Don't tell me you don't dance, she says, and puts her chin on his shoulder. At first he doesn't move at all, but eventually she feels his hand at the top of her hip and he shifts from side to side, slower than the music. He smells like clean skin and cotton spread over something sour. She closes her eyes, but before the song is over he stops and says Let's go.

Back in the truck they sit awhile. She picks at the scabs of her nail polish.

Why did you try to jump out like that? he asks.

I don't know. I was just kidding.

When she turns to the window she feels his hand on her neck, and then he starts the truck.

When she sees him for the first time she is wearing a tight sleeveless top, short skirt, and black zip-up sweater, with a pair of flats wrinkled at the heel. Her dirty blond hair and her makeup make her look older than she is but still not old enough to be in a bar.

He is sitting on the stool closest to the door, drinking beer from the bottle.

Shirley Temple, she tells the bartender, who winks at

her while topping her glass off with vodka. Three cherries bump optimistically against the ice.

Cheers, she says, turning to him. He nods, tilting his bottle.

I haven't seen you here before.

No, he says. You probably haven't.

Want to buy my next one?

He shakes his head. You shouldn't be having any.

It's only a soda, she says, and he looks away from her, sniffing. He finishes his beer in two long pulls as she watches.

Have a good night, he says, and as he is getting up to leave his eyes rest on her bare thigh. Then he is gone.

The next time they meet he is at the laundromat, fishing change from the machine. Same jeans and gray jacket. Nearly every washer is spinning as she drags her laundry bag over to him and heaves it up onto a sorting table.

Hey, she says. What are you doing here?

He looks at her like, duh.

The hose on my machine is busted, he says.

Oh. Bummer. She dumps her clothes, making a pile for underwear and socks and another for jeans, T-shirts.

How old are you? he asks.

Her head snaps up. What?

You look young.

So?

So what are you doing in bars?

She shrugs, opening a package of detergent with her teeth. She spits out a piece of plastic. I just hang out, she says.

Hang out?

Yeah, she says, slapping some clothes into a machine.

Shouldn't your mom be doing your laundry?

She gives him a hard look before slamming the machine door.

Fuck off.

He puts his hands up.

She goes out to get a burrito and when she comes back he is sitting on a bench, reading. She sits at a table where she can watch him and flips through a magazine, eating chips and pushing at some spilled beans and cheese with her finger.

What are you reading? she asks. He tilts the book forward in his lap, but she only pretends to read the title.

I bet *Cosmo* is way better, she says. *How to Please Your Man. 101 Ways.* She yawns. The edge of the plastic seat bites into her thighs and her leg goes numb.

I hate coming here, she says. It takes so long.

You got that right, he says, and gets up to check his laundry. He's good-looking, blue eyes and reddish hair, wiry body. They fold their clothes together in silence and she can tell that he is going back and forth in his mind, liking her and not.

You really shouldn't be drinking at that bar, he says, loading his clothes into a bin.

I know, she replies, and for a moment they just stand there.

Well, he says. See you.

Bye! she says, too loud, and an old woman pulling the cotton pills off a pair of socks stares, lips tight as a clothespin.

She knows he will come to the bar that night and she waits for him, holding her bottle of beer between her legs and watching a trio of boys cracking pool balls and smoking. When he comes in and stands behind her she is careful not to look at him. The hair on her neck prickles.

Are you finished with that? he asks.

Yeah. There's some backwash left if you want it, she says, not taking her eyes off the boys. Do you play pool?

No, he says, and then: Come with me.

She runs her finger through the sweat on the beer bottle. He waits.

Okay, she says, and she slips from her stool, pulling her jacket onto her arms.

Outside, they stand in front of his truck. He wipes his mouth with the back of his wrist and she sucks in her cheeks.

You haven't said anything about my outfit, she says.

It's nice. A little impractical.

She squints. You have a strange way of coming on to girls.

I'm not coming on to you.

She kicks at the gravel. Okay.

He puts his hands in his pockets, takes a few steps away from her, then turns and says Do you want to go somewhere?

He opens the door for her and slams it hard once she gets inside. There is no garbage on the floor of the cab, no empty bottles or cans, no food wrappers or old gum stuck to the dash. They drive for a long time; it's late, she's tipsy, and she falls asleep, her head slipping down the window. When she wakes up they are stopped in a steep dirt driveway and he is staring at her.

Oh, she says, wiping saliva from the side of her mouth. Where are we?

My house. Get out, he says, and then adds If you want.

She knows that they are in the foothills about an hour from town, though she doesn't know exactly where.

The house has a big porch, but that is all she can make out in the darkness. There are no neighbors.

He unlocks the door and stands aside for her to enter, reaching his hand around the jamb to flip on the light. There's an old brown couch and chair on a balding rug. Shelves filled only with books line the walls, the volumes pulled to the edges in perfect lines. A television rests on the coffee table. In the kitchen there are black pots hanging from the ceiling, a large Formica table. She checks the refrigerator: milk and brimming vegetable bins, big tub of yogurt, a brick of meat in the freezer.

Are you hungry? he asks.

No.

Then go wash your face.

What?

Upstairs. First door is the bathroom. There's an extra toothbrush in the cabinet.

He starts unloading his jacket pocket on the kitchen table. Clatter of keys and coins, the dead thump of his wallet. She stares at him.

I thought you said you weren't coming on to me.

I'm still not.

She chews the inside of her cheek.

Go on, he says.

Without another word she turns and heads up the stairs.

Take off your shoes, he calls after her, and she slips them off and drops them over the railing.

In the tiny bathroom she pees and rinses out her mouth, peeling the cellophane from the new toothbrush but leaving it unused on the rim of the sink. He knocks at the door and when she opens it he hands her a stack of blankets.

You can sleep on the couch, he tells her. It folds out.

She stares at the blankets, then back at his face. This is weird, isn't it?

Is it? he echoes. A door at the end of the hall opens and closes. She goes to the stairs and knocks the blankets around with her foot and then sits down, thinking he will come out for her in a few minutes. When she wakes up she is still there, on her back in the hallway with her socks on.

She finds him in the kitchen, an apron around his waist. Three pots tremble and spit on the stove. The air is thick with the smell of stewing fruit, and the sink, streaked with juice, is full of pits and skins.

Is that breakfast?

No.

Then what is it?

Jam, he says, pushing a jar toward her. Pot holders are over there. Hold this steady.

It takes them several minutes to get all the fruit into the jars, lined and coughing steam on the counters. She has seen people do this in movies, but wonders why anyone would do it in real life.

Who eats all this? she asks.

I do.

She begins pawing through the cabinets while he watches her. She frowns. You don't even have cereal, she says.

There's eggs.

What about lunch?

What about it?

Do you have peanut butter?

He shakes his head.

What do you eat with the jelly, then? She sighs. We need to go shopping.

He takes an envelope from the top of the refrigerator and hands it to her.

Write down what you want.

Can't I just go with you? Sometimes I don't know what I want until I see it.

No.

Well, get something good, like chips or something.

No chips.

She rolls her eyes.

Do you like fruit? he asks.

Some of it. Bananas.

Okay.

I also like ice cream, she says.

When he returns she is sitting on the back porch steps, eating a piece of bread with butter and some of the new jam. She can hear him in the house, tense footsteps upstairs and then down the hall and through the kitchen. Finally she hears the back door swing open but she doesn't turn around.

Get in the house, he says. She licks a spot of jam from her thumb.

Back already?

Did you hear me?

Calm down, she says. She pushes herself up and squeezes past his body in the doorway, her shirt tangling against his. In the kitchen she reaches into the paper sack on the table and frowns.

You didn't get any ice cream, she says, clutching a bag of mushrooms.

They didn't have any.

Idiot, she groans.

Every morning for the next three days he leaves the house for a few hours. While he is gone she watches television, or sleeps on the couch, or looks through magazines he brings her. In the evening they play cards cross-legged on the rug or at the kitchen table, Rummy and Snap and War, with the radio on to something she likes. Then he goes to bed and she stays up late watching more TV. Once while he is gone she goes to his room and opens his dresser drawers, digging beneath the neatly folded T-shirts and underwear. She finds some money, small bills, and an envelope full of receipts. She doesn't think about how many days pass or who might be missing her or what she is doing. She is just waiting for the next thing to happen.

One morning over his newspaper he says You smell like a bakery.

Like a nice French place or an outlet? she asks.

Outlet.

She looks down, pulling her shirt away from her chest. I need to get some clothes.

Now?

We could just stop by my house and I could—

No, he says.

She looks at him for a moment. Then we could go to the Goodwill, it doesn't matter. But I don't have any money. Can't we wash stuff here?

The washing machine hose is busted, he says. Remember?

Oh. Well then, I guess you're taking me out. She smiles, but he doesn't smile back, and she can see him thinking, that he is upset.

What? she asks, reaching across the table to pinch the back of his hand. He flinches. Don't you like shopping?

Outside, in the driveway, he asks her to lie down behind the bench seat of the truck.

You're joking, she says.

Just lie down there. It's clean.

Why? she asks, but he only looks at her. She waits to see if she feels scared, but she doesn't. She climbs in. On her back, with her knees drawn up, she thinks, This is really fucked up. He drives carefully so as not to bump her.

You all right? he asks.

She presses down on her skirt. I'm fine, considering, she says. The truck vibrates all the loose flesh on her body and she has to clench her teeth to keep them from rattling.

Can we have the radio at least?

He flips it on, but all they get is static.

Kandy's Super Thrift sits on a wide strip of road she has never seen before, bookended by gas stations and hamburger stands. Inside, half a dozen plastic fans whip up a breeze and a few sulky-faced girls snap gum at each other and spin the knobs on a black-and-white television.

Some dump, she says, idling through the racks, pushing at clothes that have fallen on the floor with her foot.

What do you think about this? she asks him, holding up a white top that says *I'm Your Petty Cash*.

I don't care.

She plucks a straw hat from a dented foam head. This?

Would you hurry up? he hisses.

She drops the hat and continues digging around in another row. It irritates her that he seems irritated, that he keeps his eyes on her like a giant unhappy bird. She sees a gap in the aisle, just big enough for her to fit through, and on the other side, the door.

Where do you like to shop? she asks.

He rubs his forehead.

The mall? I bet you go to the mall, she says. I bet you shop at the Gap.

You have five minutes.

Just let me try these things on, she says, holding out her arm, over which clothes are slung like slack bodies. You can come with me if you want, she adds.

No. Whatever doesn't fit I'll bring back.

She shrugs. You're paying.

You seemed older when we met, he says as they walk out to the truck. More mature.

You seemed normal, she snaps back. Less nuts.

When they get home he runs a bath while she watches.

Get in, he says.

She turns her back to him, undresses. He sits on the edge of the tub. She slips into the water.

You have a grout problem, she says, shaving her legs with his razor. It's missing in a lot of places.

Mm, he says.

Will you wash my hair?

He stares. Why?

She stares back, then shrugs. Nicer that way.

Scratching his jaw he sighs. Close your eyes, he says, and kneels beside the tub.

She leans forward, her chin on her knees. He scrubs shampoo in circles over her head, his thumbs hard against her scalp. He does the conditioner, then puts one hand on her forehead and the other on the back of her neck and lays her down flat in the gray water.

Rinse, he says, the ceiling light bright behind his head. From beneath the water she looks straight up into his face. When she is finished he squeezes her hair into a rope that drips over her shoulder.

You're all set, he says.

As she gets out of the tub water slops over the porcelain and onto the floor. She stands in front of him, water slowing in the hair between her legs. He reaches up to touch her face. She opens her lips and he pushes two fingers past them and as she closes her eyes she thinks, *Now.* But she is wrong.

Because she wins the next night's game of Rummy she is allowed to have one beer.

Toast me, she says, lying next to him on the living-room rug. She tips the neck of her bottle toward his.

No chance, he says. You cheated.

She laughs and forces the lip of her beer into his. When she is finished drinking she turns toward him, propping herself up on her elbow, her fist against her cheek.

So where do you work? she asks.

Slaughterhouse.

Oh, she says. She can't tell whether he is joking or not. Do you have a girlfriend?

He shakes his head.

Why not?

He shrugs. Just don't.

You have me, though.

He grunts, taking a long swallow of beer. She scoots closer to him.

Your hair is in my face, he says. She leans down to kiss him and he kisses her back. She tastes alcohol and that night's spaghetti sauce. His eyes are closed for a moment but when she lifts her leg and spreads it over his hip, reaching for the zipper on his jeans, he puts his hand on her chest.

Stop, he says, sitting up.

Why?

Because.

Don't you like me?

I like you, he says, rubbing his eyebrows. I like you.

Why, then? Why not?

He gets up and takes the bottles to the kitchen, throwing them into the trash so hard they crack. She follows him in, hands on her hips, and he turns to her and says Don't you know anyone who doesn't want to fuck you?

She flinches. *You're* the one who brought me here! she shouts. We do the same things every day and you never want to go anywhere and I have to lie down in your stupid truck on the *floor* and you make me—

I don't *make* you do anything, he cuts in, flinging the back door open. You want to go? Get out.

Fuck you! she screams, kicking the door shut so hard the windows rattle in their frames. His face twitches.

What's wrong with you? she says. He looks away.

It's late. You should go to bed.

Would you stop telling me what to do?

———

Early the next morning she goes to his room. He is lying on his side beneath the sheets, one rough cheek resting on his bicep. Everywhere there is cracking plaster, more bookshelves, the painted dresser with its drawers shut tight. Water and a cluster of keys stand on a little table beside his bed. Everything feels familiar to her but also strange, because she sees so clearly the pieces but not how they fit together.

Come here, he says.

I thought you were sleeping.

No. I don't sleep very well.

She shuffles toward him until the backs of her hands brush against the mattress. He makes room for her and she lies on her side next to him, her breasts chafing against her T-shirt.

He touches her eyebrow with his thumb. I'm sorry I made you lie in the back of the truck.

It's okay. She tries to look him in the eye but she can't.

Go to sleep, he says, and somehow she does.

When she wakes up he is gone. She rinses her underwear and shirts in the kitchen sink and when he comes home he sees her clothes slung over the shower rod, dripping on the floor, and he stops and says Didn't I tell you I fixed the washer?

———————

That evening he says he wants to go for a walk. Outside, it's still light. It's too cold, she says, stopping at the bottom of the porch, but he doesn't turn around.

You should have put on a sweater.

She throws her hands up. This is exactly what I'm talking about. You always want to do something that doesn't make any *sense*. She considers turning back, but instead kicks at a rock and keeps going.

They walk about a mile and then there is a loud cracking noise, like a gunshot.

What's that?

Just a branch, he says. We can go back now if you want.

No, she says.

We can.

No, she says again. Chase me.

He looks at her.

Come on, she urges.

Okay, he says. Run.

She takes off into the trees.

As soon as she knows she is out of sight she stops, leaning against a tree, the air on her lips brittle as she catches her breath. The sky is hooded with leaves and where the sun melts through it turns the dust in the air to gold.

You're fast, he says, coming up behind her. She stumbles away from the tree.

Shit, she says, still panting. You scared me.

Should we go back?

Not yet.

Then what now?

She smiles. Now you have to kill me.

He pushes his hands into his pockets.

Yeah?

Yeah.

And what if I want you to kill me?

She blinks. What?

Go ahead, he says.

She reaches out and touches his stomach with the palm of her hand, running it up to his chest and then down past his belt while he watches her. She wonders about beauty, about the way he looks right now—older and folded in on himself—and the heat in her body that will not stop.

Aren't you going to hit me? he says.

Her hands slide off him and she takes a small step sideways.

Don't be scared, he says.

I'm not, she says.

Then hit me. He lifts his chin. Come on.

I can't.

Yes you can.

When she sees him raise his hand she thinks for a moment that she should try to stop him, but she doesn't and he hits her, hard, across her face, knocking her to her knees. He crouches down behind her, an arm wrapped tight around her waist.

What do you want? he asks.

Tell me I'm beautiful, she says.

You're beautiful, he says into her ear, and then again into her hair. You're beautiful. Her shoulders start to shake.

Listen to me, he says. You have to go home.

No.

You have to.

No, she says, sinking her fingers into the ground.

When I count to ten, he says. One. Two.

Why? she whispers. I don't want to.

But he keeps counting. And when he gets to ten he lets her go.

LOVE, LUCY

Did you do that? he asked, his hands on his hips, squinting, as I held up the pigeon for him to see. It was the first thing I killed. I was four. I dropped the bird at his feet.

You didn't mean to, he said.

I kicked the bird and it bounced off the front door, leaving a rich red smear. One of its eyes, pried loose by a butter knife, fell out. I had stabbed it all over. He pretended not to notice.

We'll give it a nice burial, he said.

I snatched the bird and shook it. I gnashed my teeth and made dying sounds and sailed the corpse over the porch railing, where it splashed into the dirt. I smeared

my fingers down the front of his shirt, leaving behind
ten wet tracks branching over the cotton, delicate as
a Japanese painting. My hands were small then. He
held them, he kissed them; animal blood touched his
mouth. I howled, I hissed, trying to free myself from
his grip.

It's a phase, he decided. But I had just begun.

When he found me in the toolshed, so the story goes, I
was covered in black fur. He was already an old man,
widowed early, childless; he figured, Finders keepers.
He trimmed me with scissors and kept the hair in a box
on which he wrote *Lucy Fur.*

Now when did you hear of a kid having fur? That's
what I call special, he'd say.

He brought the box out sometimes and let me play
with it. The hair felt like a cat's. I could imagine his
fingers straying over me, lifting and cutting. When I
smelled the box I smelled ashes.

He had to block the front door when a friend stopped
by for a beer or to say hello. *I'm sorry*, he'd say, *but she
bites*, and I would bark, loud. If you wanted to see him
you'd have to find him somewhere I wasn't. Even the
porch was off-limits; when the postman came I jabbed
at him through the door slot with a pair of scissors.

But my not-father didn't complain. He didn't want to go out. I've had enough of drinking and women, he'd say, and turn the television on to his favorite show—the one he'd named me after—while I sat beside him, picking holes in the green velveteen and pulling the stuffing through until the cushion on my side of the couch was empty and I had to sit on the floor.

When I was five I took a stick and wrote in the sand, I AM THE SON OF THE DEVIL. We were at the beach. I was not crazy about the waves or the seaweed. He was gathering shells and I pointed at the words with my stick and he turned his head to the side to read them.

Okay, he said, shaking scallops in his palm. A, you're a girl. B, do I look like the devil?

I took the stick again. *You*, I wrote, and then I drew an equal sign with a slash through it, followed by *My dad*.

He sighed. You sore about being adopted?

I jabbed the stick into the sand and threw myself down on the picnic blanket, my back to him. I could hear him unwrapping the sandwiches he took from his pockets. My stomach growled.

Come on, he said, reaching around my shoulder with a piece of ham. Even devil spawn has to eat.

I chomped at his fingers. He burped behind me, wiping his hands in the sand.

There was no one else on the beach. It was cold and gray. Still, he swam. He pulled me out into the water. I sank. He pulled me back up. My hair gleamed like black oil around my shoulders and he scooped it up in his hands like treasure.

You are beautiful, he said. I punched him in the arm. He twisted to his knees with a splash, grinning. I wondered sometimes if he was senile. With the water licking his waist he looked up at me.

Someone lost the lottery the day they lost you, but I won it, he said. Which was wrong. Which didn't even make sense. But he believed it.

I was expelled from school for putting tacks in the rain boots lined up in the coatroom. He said he never liked that stupid school to begin with. It became my job to fix the rotten wood porch, to pull weeds by the fence, to peel potatoes. I did everything wrong, but he still said Good job, Lucy! whenever I presented him with a handful of torn-up violets or showed him the porch pounded too full of nails or the potatoes hacked to pieces. In the evenings, I waited in the kitchen for bugs to crawl past so I could stomp on them with both feet, thinking *Kill kill kill*.

Did you get them all? he'd call, and I'd jump in response, making the windows rattle in their loose frames.

Thatta girl, he'd say.

———

I was seven, smashing a square block against a round hole in a puzzle he'd made as a Christmas present. I hated Christmas presents. After an hour of smashing he grabbed my arm and yelled Lucy, use the other damn block!

I went rigid; it was the first time he'd yelled at me. The square fell out of my hand. Immediately he knelt beside me, offering the block on his big palm.

I'm sorry I said damn, he said. Go on doing it your own way.

I was still for a moment, then pushed all the pieces into their proper slots as fast as I could. We looked at the puzzle together in silence. Then I shoved it over and went to my room, which was his room, too. I pulled the sheets over my head and breathed out hard to make a tent. He stuck his face in. I slapped it. He sang. I put my hands over my ears. The song was supposed to be funny. *Ha* was not a sound I could make, just as I could not say *hello* or *please* or my name, or any name. I could not tell him he was driving me crazy, and he couldn't take a hint. So he kept singing.

When I was ten I started menstruating. How about that, he said when he saw the stain blooming on the crotch of my jeans. You want me to get you some sanitary thingamajigs? he offered, but I insisted on bleeding anywhere and everywhere, like an animal, staining the couch, the carpet, the tile. My skin flared. My chest was always sore and I wore his clothes, T-shirts that came to my knees, pants rolled fat at my ankles and cinched at the waist with rope. I wanted robes, a crown; but it was not my time yet. Instead, I ran through the fields barefoot, my toenails black, my arms out like wings. I waited in trees, savaging the leaves and pinching ants between my fingers; when he passed beneath me I dropped onto his shoulders and he grunted like nothing bigger than a softball had hit him, reaching back to catch my shins. I made a sign asking what was for dinner. Spaghetti, he said, and I thumped the side of his head. Sloppy Joes, he offered, and I hit him again; he chortled and said Okay okay, liver and onions it is. I licked my chops.

At twelve I was asked to a dance by a boy. I knew by his good looks and sideways eyes that my not-father had put him up to asking me. Instead of going, I burned the old dance hall down to the ground. There were people inside, but they managed to get out more or less intact before the roof fell in. Flames flew from the burst windows as glass flocked the lawn and shrieks dressed the night sky. I was watching from a tree and he pulled me by my foot from the branch, quiet, making sure no one saw me.

Sit down, he said, once we were home and he'd locked the door just in case. I would not sit down. He sighed.

I taught you better than to go fooling with matches. A fire can be real dangerous.

I waved my arms to say, I know!

Someone could get hurt.

I grinned to show I meant it. He rubbed his eye.

Lucy, he said, you don't have to do none of these bad things.

I nodded that yes, I did, and yes, I would.

No, you don't. You're a good girl.

I shook my head until my hair flew. The room spun. He wanted to get hold of me; I crashed away. In a corner he reached for my shoulders. I butted my head into his soft stomach. I pushed and pushed. He held the tops of my arms.

You can't make me not care for you, he said. So you should go on and quit trying.

I kept pushing. He dipped his head down to mine, his torso curving to protect me instead of himself. We became a shell inside a shell, the insides of us never touching, but the outsides as close as two outsides could be.

You can't hurt me, he said.

I dug my feet into the floor; I pressed my hands into his chest. I became a bull. Maybe for minutes, maybe for hours. But he was strong, and I was still a girl, coated in weakness like a caul. I fell asleep against his stomach. When I woke up his arms were crossed, heavy, over my back; he was snoring, his cheek on my head. I opened my eyes and my lashes kissed the belly of his T-shirt.

The next morning he slung a hammock from two posts on the porch. From then on in the bed we'd shared I was alone. I wrestled from one cold end to the other; I took to sleeping on the floor. Dust clung to my hair like dirt in the weave of a broom. He had to haul me up by the elbows in the morning while I made my body into dead weight. At breakfast I insisted on eating my bacon raw, my elbows on the table, my hair pooling in my plate. He let me eat until I threw up, and then he cleaned the mess I made.

Later a friend or relative called asking how I was and he said Well she's at that age. Weird diets and always aching for a fight.

I slunk around the kitchen doorway and stared at him.

I have to go now, he said. Lucy's trying to give me the creeps.

He hung up, turned to me. You feeling any better? he asked. I hissed. He handed me a glass of milk.

In the months before I turned thirteen I was transformed. The muscles stood out on my arms; my bones sharpened and stretched. All over I became hard, like the rocks I dug out of the riverbeds and smashed against the branches. We arm-wrestled on the porch. He pretended he was letting me win.

Out in the fields I tore my clothes to shreds. I stayed out all night; he kept the porch lights burning and let me sleep until evening. When I shuffled out of my room for dinner he wanted to play cards. I yawned into my elbow and looked at my hand, playing for spades no matter what the game was. Finally he gave up, gathering the deck and grumbling You can't just make it up as you go along, that's why there's rules.

I crammed the last sausage into my mouth.

You gonna dry these dishes? he asked as he washed them; licking grease from my fingers I nodded yes, but as soon as he turned his back I slipped out the door, hungry for the dark, the house bright behind me as I ran.

I could have done it with my mind. Tools were beneath me; they were things that any creature could use, and I was no longer bound by human laws. I could have done it from far away, while he was sleeping, in a split second. But I wanted him to see it coming.

Oh, that's a big knife you got there, he said, swinging in the hammock. It was midnight; he'd been waiting up for me. I crept toward him, the porch light cutting either side of the knife I held so tight in my hand.

That knife's not for playing, honey-Lucy.

I am grown, I wanted to scream. *I know what are toys and what are not.* I came close to him, close enough to see the wrinkles squeezed out by the corners of his eyes as he smiled.

I lifted the knife. He leaned way back to look at me, his not-daughter who had suddenly grown so tall, and in the dark rooms of his pupils I saw that I, too, had become dark.

You love me, he said, and reaching for my face, he touched his knuckle to my chin. I raised my face as high as I could, but his arms were long and he stayed touching me.

He was never scared of me. Even then. He watched as I brought the knife down.

Afterward I went from room to room, touching the things he had touched for the past thirteen years: one by one every object shattered and broke, snapped and collapsed. The couch, his chair, the bed, the broom. The television spat glass and smoke. The curtains turned to dust. Back on the porch I laid his body on the boards, and I dissolved the hammock, burst his bottle of beer. The house had black eyes for windows, a hole for a mouth; then it, too, was gone. At last I reached for him, and he ran through my fingers like molten gold, glittering my palms with ash.

I have no eyes anymore, or eyelashes. There are no more shirts, or bellies, or breath, or birds, or blood; there are no seas, or sheets; there are no animals, and there are no masters of animals. These things are gone, along with the rest of the beauty of the world, which I despised, and only I remain, reigning over all I have unmade, the last bad daughter, free of all proud fathers.

HEARTBREAKER

There's a party at Melissa's. The door is open and some people are sitting on the porch steps drinking vodka shots from plastic cups. Natalie gets a beer from the cooler and sits on the couch in the living room. Some guy is standing in front of the only working fan with his shirt puffed out over it, and when he sees her looking at him he raises his cup and smiles.

What's up? he says.

Natalie shrugs. I don't know, she says. Nothing.

After two beers she walks home, her toes blistering in her shoes. It's nine o'clock but it's still hot and the sky is bright purple. Boredom is like a virus wrestling in her stomach and her jaw aches from what the boy at the party did to her, taking his time; she almost fell asleep. She wonders if her neighbors have any weed they will give her.

On her street she sees Frog riding his skateboard, smiling his stupid smile. She doesn't know what's wrong with him exactly that he smiles like that, like a dog, at everything and everybody, even when someone is calling him Faggot or Freak or Frog, or messing with his skateboard, threatening to kick his ass.

Hey Frog, she says. Remember me? Natalie?

Yeah, yeah, he says, blinking like he has something in his eye. Hi!

How are you?

Good, he says. He gulps when he talks, his lips wet and open. She lifts the hair off the back of her neck, then lets it drop back down again.

It's kind of late to be out skating, she says.

I have to practice, Frog says.

For what, the Special Olympics?

He blinks.

Can you jump off that curb? she asks, pointing to the end of her street.

Yeah! Frog shouts, and he takes off, his sneaker

pushing hard against the concrete, flipping the board up and over; for a moment he is in the air, his arms flung out, the board spinning below him, and then both he and the board land together.

Did you see? he shouts from the end of the street, breathing hard.

Yeah, she yells back. That was really good.

You want to try? he asks, skating back. She shakes her head.

I have to go. But I'll see you around, okay?

Okay, he says, Bye, and she can feel him watch her walk away.

She is starting her sophomore year again because she missed too much class the year before and flunked out. Sitting at the scarred wooden desk, she feels giant, over-grown, though she is the same size as everyone else. She has to be asked twice to give her name in Spanish class. When people talk it's like trying to hear something underwater. From her desk she can see the portable classroom buildings where they have the special ed for Frog and the wheelchair kid and the girl who got burned and wears a hat all the time. If Natalie fucks this year up maybe they'll put her with the freaks and she can drool and eat Goldfish crackers and play with puzzles all day.

Do you ever wonder what it's like to be retarded? she asks Melissa in the cafeteria line.

No, Melissa says, but I bet it would suck. I mean, right?

I guess, Natalie says, taking a package of chips from a basket, then putting it back. But maybe you'd be too stupid to know. Maybe it's just like being a little kid your whole life.

You can't be so stupid that you don't know you're retarded, Melissa says.

Good point, Natalie says, and laughs.

After school she stops by the 7-Eleven. She sees Frog's mom getting a drink from the fountain machine. Natalie stands right next to her, going through the magazines, but Mrs. Hoff doesn't turn her head. She watches as the woman, overweight in a defiant sort of way, takes her change and her cigarettes and her Big Gulp and walks out to the parking lot, sucking up soda through the straw.

You can't read those if you're not going to pay for them, the man tells the girl.

I have money, Natalie says, angry, taking a magazine and dropping it on the counter. She looks out the window in time to see Mrs. Hoff get into her car, the skirt of the woman's dress catching in the door when she slams it shut.

She ends up at Frog's house an hour later. She knocks, loud, then stands back on the porch with her hands on her hips, chewing gum. Mrs. Hoff comes to the door and sticks her head out.

Yeah, she says, her eyes sleepy, a cigarette between her fingers.

Is Frog home?

Mrs. Hoff squints. Frog?

I mean Christopher.

Yeah, why?

I want to talk to him, she says, shrugging.

Chris! Mrs. Hoff yells, and turning away she leaves the door open, so that Natalie can see the light from a television flickering on the hallway wall.

Hi, he says, smiling that crazy smile.

Hi, she says. Did you miss me?

Yeah.

I wanted to give you a present, she says, leaning forward.

A present?

For your birthday.

My birthday's next month! he almost shouts.

It's an early present, she says. Because we're friends.

Thanks, Frog says, spitting a little. He wipes his lips. Sorry, he adds.

Do you want to know what it is?

He nods. Natalie glances behind Frog into the house, then looks back at him, into his big pale eyes.

You have to promise not to tell. It's a secret.

Promise, he says quickly.

She pulls out a magazine from a plastic bag and hands it to him.

Oh, he says as the magazine falls open. In the centerfold a woman lies on a bed, her hand between her legs. Frog stares.

Natalie smiles. Nice, huh?

He keeps on staring.

You like it? she asks, spitting her gum over the end of the concrete porch.

Yeah, he says. She looks at his crotch.

Are you getting a hard-on, Frog?

He keeps staring at the photo, the way Natalie sometimes does in math class, like if he looks long enough the answer will magically appear.

You can use it, for later, she says. Now hide it before your mom sees.

He just looks at her.

Never mind, she says, taking the magazine from him. When you want to see it you can come to my house, okay?

Yeah, Frog says, staring at the bag as she tucks the magazine away. His face is as smooth as an eggshell, no scars, no acne, not even freckles.

You're lucky, she says, and he says, Yeah.

The next day, a Saturday, she gets the magazine out from under her bed. She lies down with her back to the door and examines a spread showing two women in red lingerie kissing. In the back of the magazine there are ads for penis pumps and blow-up dolls and phone sex. She dials one of the 800 numbers and listens to a girl's voice asking her for her credit card information. She hangs up, then lifts the receiver again and calls 411 to ask for Chris Hoff's number. She writes it on her hand.

Hello, he answers.

Frog?

I'm Chris, he says.

Duh, she says. Is your mom home?

No, he says.

Good. She turns over on her back, the phone tucked under her chin. What are you doing?

Watching TV.

What are you watching?

SpongeBob, he says.

Sponge what?

It's my favorite show! he says.

She sighs. I wish I had a favorite show. I'm bored.

Yeah, he says.

Are you thinking about me? she asks, her legs propped up on her windowsill, staring at the blunt ugly concrete of the neighbor's house an arm's length away. He doesn't say anything, just breathes into the phone.

Did you think about me today? she repeats.

Um, he says.

Did you touch yourself?

Huh?

I want you to stop acting so stupid, she says. I asked you a question.

I'm not *stu*pid. He says it like something his mother taught him to say, like *Please* or *No thank you*.

Don't be mad, she says, I was just kidding.

Okay, he says.

Why do you think I talk to you? she asks. She pushes her foot through the open window and out into the air and waits.

You called me, he says.

You're right, she says, I did, and she hangs up.

She goes to the kitchen to make dinner: her mother is standing by the sink, in her robe with her hair in a towel, drinking coffee.

Who was on the phone? her mother asks.

Chris Hoff, Natalie says.

Her mother frowns. Doesn't he have Down syndrome or something?

Natalie shrugs. I don't know what he's got. She puts a bag of popcorn in the microwave and watches it swell with steam.

But he's got something wrong, her mother says.

I guess, yeah.

She takes the popcorn out of the microwave and dumps it into a bowl. She eats it standing up next to the sink while her mother looks at her.

I got a job, you know, her mother says, lifting her chin.

Great, she replies, licking butter from her fingers.

I don't know why you want to be making friends with retards.

Even retards need friends, Natalie says.

She watches an episode of *Cops*, during which a black girl punches a white girl during Mardi Gras and the white one spits out a tooth. She sucks her own front teeth, which aren't bad considering she's never been to the dentist, and then she fumbles around in a pile of dirty clothes for a lip gloss.

Mom, she yells, I'm going out, and the front door slams behind her.

———

She walks along his driveway to the back of his house, through the white iron gate stuttering on a broken hinge. She's not even trying to be quiet, but nobody hears the dry grass cracking under her feet. She looks through his bedroom window; a poster of a cartoon character and some skateboard stickers are stuck to the wall. He's sleeping in his jeans with the lights on, his sneakers filthy on the blanket. After a while Mrs. Hoff comes in with a microwave dinner. He eats it there on the bed, by himself, sometimes using a plastic fork, sometimes his fingers. When he drinks his milk his Adam's apple jumps. He wipes his mouth with the neck of his shirt and when he's finished eating he looks at the wall, his mouth open. His mother doesn't come back in. At one point he laughs, a single hard sound. She taps on his window but it's too dark for him to see her and he just stares at the glass, looking at himself.

The next night she waits for him at dusk, walking the block back and forth and listening for the sound of his skateboard. Soon enough he comes out of his house, arms flung out at his sides.

Hi you, she says. He stops, holding his board by the lip, breathing hard through his mouth.

Hi.

Where are you going?

Nowhere, he says.

You wanna come over to my house? Hang out?

She takes his hand, which is damp but cool, almost rubbery. His fingers are limp. She squeezes.

You can bring your skateboard, she says. Come on.

She leads him down the street and into her dark house. As she opens her bedroom door Frog stops.

It's okay, she says, just relax, and he follows her inside. They stumble over clothes and shoes as she takes him to her bed and they sit side by side, their knees touching.

I bet you've been waiting to see this again, Natalie says, and slides the magazine out from under her pillow.

Yeah, he says.

We can share, she says, opening the magazine over their laps. You tell me which one you like best.

She turns the pages. Frog stares, his head moving slowly as she directs him to each new page.

How about this one? she asks, and he nods and says, Yeah.

What do you like about her?

She has pretty hair, he says.

What about her pussy? Do you like that?

Yeah.

You want to fuck her?

Yeah.

You ever seen a girl without her clothes on? Not in a magazine, but a real girl?

No? he says, like a question. She laughs. He's like a plant, alive but volitionless; she can't see any sign that he is actually thinking. This is kind of sad to her, but also kind of funny. He smells like corn chips.

You just sit there, she says, and I'll show you.

She pushes the magazine to the floor and stands up. She pulls her top over her head, then steps out of her skirt, forgetting the hole in her underwear, the torn lace on her bra. She starts grinding her hips, arching her back, flipping her hair, humming. She does all the things she's wanted to do with other guys but felt too embarrassed to: dance, pose, put her head back, touch herself.

You're pretty, Frog says.

Thank you, Natalie says, and her smile is genuine. She goes down on her knees and looks him in the eye, close enough to see the dandruff in his hair, the baby fuzz clustered around his lips.

What do you think? she asks, opening his knees a little so she can slip between them. You want to see more? She puts his hand to her breast, squeezing her fingers over his. His body goes rigid.

It's okay, she croons. Here, look. She starts to unhook her bra and then slips the straps over her shoulders, slow, before letting it fall to the floor.

See? she says, reaching out to touch him, but he flinches and turns his head.

I said it's *okay*, she says, grabbing for his hand, trying to pull him back to her, but he screeches, like a cat or a bird, and she lets go.

I go home, I go home! he cries, cowering, a bubble of snot hanging from his nose.

Get out, then, you fucking idiot, she hisses, throwing her jacket at his head. His nose keeps running and he doesn't wipe it. Get out, she says again, and he scrambles to the door. She follows him, mostly naked, her hair swinging in her face.

You forgot your board, dumbass! she yells, and he stops and looks at her, his eyes glittering in the dark, his red mouth distorted by fear and stupidity, still smiling.

Natalie brushes her hair until it crackles. Her mascara has dried up; she plunges the wand in and out of the tube, then throws it against the wall. Cheap shit, she says to herself, and puts on more eyeliner.

She goes to Melissa's. It's Thursday and there are twenty people there, maybe more. She gets sucked into a kitchen full of boys. The table is covered in beer bottles, ashtrays, exploding bags of chips; someone's brother just turned twenty-one and there is a sheet cake that people are eating with their fingers.

Hey Felicia, one guy says as she walks to the table, grabbing a handful of Doritos.

I'm not Felicia, she says.

Oh, he says. No one gets up for her to sit down so she just leans against the stove while they talk. She gets bored hearing about TV, movies, other girls. Everyone is talking at the same time. For a while it's like she's turned into a zombie, not really thinking anything, her body numb. She lets her eyes go out of focus so that everything blurs together and for a moment she thinks she knows what it's like to just not exist. Then someone bumps into her arm and she snaps out of it.

Do you have a cigarette? she asks no one in particular. A boy fumbles in his pocket, shaking his head.

You have to start bringing your own shit, he says, and Natalie rolls her eyes, taking the cigarette he offers.

You know that retard at school? Frog? she says, taking a drag. Her shirt rides up over her hip, exposing a strip of skin and bone.

Oh man, someone says, slapping his jeans. That guy's fucking hilarious.

They all take turns imitating Frog's expression, the

way he talks, his loose-armed way of walking, until they're hysterical with laughter.

Well, she cuts in, blowing cigarette smoke to the ceiling. I fucked him.

Everyone stops talking.

Damn, one guy says, leaning back in his chair.

Serious? another guy asks.

Yeah, she says.

What's his dick like?

Like a *dick*, idiot. He's retarded, not deformed.

The table is quiet for a moment; then she winks, and they grin and laugh and get more drinks and drink them and she goes into the backyard with someone: but right before it happens she pulls her arm from his grip and says No, I don't want to, and the boy is slapping at her clothes but she slaps right back until he is off her, cursing. Melissa calls to her from the porch, but Natalie shakes her head and walks fast, her arms around her waist; when she is home she sits down hard on her bed, swallowing, pressing her palms to her eyes until it hurts.

Frog, she says on the phone, into his answering machine. It's me.

What do you want? Mrs. Hoff says, picking up the phone, and the girl is too startled for a moment to say anything.

What? Mrs. Hoff repeats.

I want to talk to Frog, the girl says. Where is he?

At a friend's.

A *friend's*? Natalie says. She is lashed by jealousy, rage. She clenches the phone until her knuckles go white.

He can't talk to you, Mrs. Hoff says, and hangs up.

It's almost noon by the time she gets to school. She doesn't have her books or her backpack; her hair is uncombed, her top from the night before wrinkled and stained under the arms. As she cuts through the main building, she sees that someone has written on her locker in black marker *Natalie Harper fucks retards.*

She punches through the heavy double doors and strides toward the special ed bungalow at the back of the field. Soon the bell will ring for lunch and there will be students everywhere, streaming across the hot grass. But for now it's just Natalie, and the bungalow, and Frog's face through the window, turned toward a piece of paper on his desk.

Chris! she shouts, slapping an open palm against the glass. *Chris!*

He lifts his head, looking first in the wrong direction, then catching her eye. She's hitting the thick glass so hard she can feel it vibrating in her elbow, her shoulder; she must look crazy, she thinks, with her bad hair and ugly clothes, her fist coming down again and again, but he just smiles, a smile so wide it swallows her, it breaks her heart.

STILETTO

The garage belongs to my father. We—three half brothers, not a single mother in common—work for cash stuffed in envelopes and pinned to a board next to the refrigerator. I am the shortest of my siblings by far, my head not even hoping to graze their chins. When they want to describe how small something is—a mini-fridge, an enemy's penis—they say it is *Robert-size*. Among us brothers there are meth addictions, adult acne, and missing teeth, but my height is the crown jewel of our misfortunes, so constantly, awfully funny that my brothers have to choke back laughter every time they see me, even though they see me almost every day, even though, at 5'1", I am technically not a midget but merely below average. A distinction lost on them. On everyone.

Where I live is what they call a "garden" apartment; it sits mostly belowground, damp, low-ceilinged. *Perfect for you!* the landlord bellowed when he showed it to me, and it is perfect—not because of the ceilings, but because of the single dim window above my bed. Through it I see STILETTO. I also see dog paws—dog shit—bicycle tires—sneakers—rubber—pure sidewalk. My window grows filthy with cigarette ash and piss. Trash caresses the glass, twitching in between the bars of the iron grate, a sensual shudder mirroring my own as I wait for STILETTO to walk by. Her passing lasts a miraculous three seconds, slow enough for me to see what I want to see, fast enough to keep me hoping for more: skin, muscle, tendon, bone, the briefest flash of a blister above the patent lip of her high high heel.

After I see STILETTO I do this to myself: my foot up on the back of the sink, the razor skimming down and down, down and in. The blood goes in fat lines to the drain, some to the floor. The whole time I'm cutting I'm also saying *Fuckfuckfuck*: then I drop the blade, rinse my fingers, and turn on the water. I wrap a white towel over my ankle and knot it tight.

I wish I could explain this to you, what I'm doing,

why I'm doing it. I've tried all the short man's voodoo: lifts in my shoes—stretching—vitamins—diets. My brothers just laughed harder. And now I think, there's already so little of me, what's a little less? Pain is not the point, though it tags along.

At work I can barely walk. In the kitchen I pour some coffee and Dad says What are you, drunk? I shake my head, one hand on my stomach, and drink my coffee. It's agony trying to ease myself down on the creeper but once I'm off my feet the pain simmers down to a dull constant throb. I can feel my pant leg hitched up and I know the bandages are showing. Carl stops at my feet and says What the fuck, dude. Then his boots move on. When I know the coast is clear I roll out, go inside to use the bathroom. Carl can probably fill the mirror over the sink with his reflection. Not me. Just my face and the top of my shoulders show. But I'm not looking in the mirror, I'm unwinding the bandage, which is stained through. The wound is sticking to the bandage and it will hurt if I peel it off now so I don't, I just rewind the bandage tight, trying not to inhale the sickish-sweet odor that rises from it. Ray bangs on the door, says he has to piss. I ignore him. The bathroom window looks out onto an ordinary street, residential, clean, empty—it means nothing to me. Most windows don't, most feet don't. It's not like I'm some kind of fetishist. Or if I am, it's a new thing, it happened since the apartment, since STILETTO, and it's not my fault. The thought of holding a razor now makes me feel sick. But I know I'll go home and I'll see her and then the razor will seem harmless, will seem good, and I'll be right back where I started.

I bend down, unroll the cuff on my pant leg, and open the door.

Christ, I thought you'd fallen in and we'd have to fish your ass out, Ray says, shoving my head, and I am so tired I don't even tell him to go fuck himself, I just slide back under a car and stay there.

On payday I come home and find my envelope short $20. I count the bills over and over—we are paid in ones and fives—and then I sit staring at the envelope, chewing my cheek. I hobble to the phone and dial my father's number. Take it or leave it, he says, and hangs up. I hit the receiver against the wall and am surprised when it breaks, plastic shooting under the fridge, clattering across the stove. There is only room for one person in the kitchen, and when I stand still in the middle I can touch the fridge, the sink, and the oven without taking a step. It's a shithole, I realize, this kitchen, this apartment. I eat some SpaghettiOs out of the pot. My ankle flares.

Outside the window traffic is heavy and I am road-kill beneath it all night long.

On Monday, a workday, a miracle: lying prone beneath the corroded belly of a Ford I hear the click-clack I'd only ever heard through glass approaching in full stereo—STILETTO coming straight toward me! I am breathless, instantly hard, terrified. I am a panicked dog in its cage hoping for a kick.

Carl, she calls. Carl!

What's her voice like? Like your mother threatening to take something away from you.

You've had it since eight yesterday morning, she says, and I realize that the clean midprice Saab convertible just a few feet away from me belongs to *her*—how could I not have guessed it, the gleaming black paint job a perfect echo of STILETTO's heels.

I told you it'll be ready at six, Carl whisper-whines, and I flinch again, because he knows her, *knows*, maybe not quite fucking her, but almost? Or wants to? Or used to want to? She is Dad's age—it's in her voice, the skin on her feet—and Carl is almost handsome, long hair bleached yellow, though all of our hair is naturally brown: their shoes are so close together, the brutal steel-toed boots, the teetering heels.

I can't take the bus back, she says, and he sighs. I

hear his hand run through his hair, I hear his hair fall back over his eye.

There's a Starbucks two blocks down, why don't you wait and it will be done in an hour, he says. I see the toe of one shoe lift as STILETTO stretches her Achilles, a gesture of consideration, impatience; finally she agrees, though not before saying that it isn't worth the deal Carl's giving her, it's no deal if Carl can't do something simple on time. I know Carl is less than interested in her complaint—he must have made the promise to her long ago, not expecting it to be cashed in—and I think *You stupid fucking bastard Carl*. I watch STILETTO walk back down the drive, tight steps hobbled by a tight skirt, and I braid my arms deep in the guts of the Ford's undercarriage.

Dad's boots come down the backdoor steps. What's it need? he barks, and Carl *pffs*. Fucking oil, he says. Dad says You're an idiot and Ray laughs from the lawn, where he is messing with a dead engine. I'm done with the Ford—I hardly have any work to do all day—but I stay beneath it. Carl tests the Saab and I listen; it hums. Dad's fist raps the hood of my car. YOU GOT THAT RUNNING GOOD, ROBERT? he yells and I feel myself draining into the bandages as I shout YES SIR.

Carl finishes with the oil and bangs the hood of the car shut. Vacuum, he orders, and drops the Shop-Vac at my feet. While he eats his lunch on the porch step

I vacuum STILETTO's car with ruthless precision. The floor mat below her pedals is an especially tender area and I stroke the nozzle over every nook and cranny, the vacuum's hungry sucking music to my ears. I polish the pedals with a damp cloth, Windex the glass on the dashboard. I could lick the steering wheel—the pedals— the pale leather seats—there are so many temptations to resist. For a moment, for many moments, I refrain. But in the end I am only human.

The rear door opens with a click. I get in, coil on the floor behind the driver's seat. I breathe. Already my back aches. With my dark hair, my dark clothes, pressed against the dark carpet, I might be a backpack or a duffel bag, a dropped cloth. I wait.

Less than an hour later I hear STILETTO approach, her heels *cawk-cawking* as she steps up to the kitchen door and calls for Carl. There's a muffled conversation about payment; I can almost hear the sound of STILETTO's money being crushed in Carl's greasy fist. Then she opens the car door and her body slides into place, displacing lesser molecules, and I turn my nose toward the floor so I can get a better look, my whole body tuning itself to this vision: the wink of patent leather against flesh. The slamming of the door, the car ON; I am made of flames. STILETTO's high heel, indented minutely—by gravel, or stones—nails the mat as she depresses the gas. I'm doing it wildly, my hand between my legs, the sound of the road eating the sound of my terrible pleasure. Did she notice how I polished her steering wheel, sucked the dust from her console—the cup holder—the coin tray? Fuck Carl, I could be her mechanic for life. She turns on the radio—voices, not music—and the turn signal *click click clicks*. Shadows are passing over me, caressing me—trees, buildings, streetlights—and I shiver beneath them, a hunchback, a fetus, curled so tight, my eyes narrowed and burning. And the air rancid with her perfume.

She parks somewhere quiet. Still. Complete stillness. The engine ticks down. Suburb? Which one? Without the sound of the road, without the radio, I have to be quiet; I hold my breath. She's waiting for something. I inch my hand, wet, under the seat; I can sense her weight through the sag of the springs, and her nearness radiates like an X-ray right through me.

Maybe it's a minute that she stays here, part of the air she is breathing my air, part of her body a part, in a way, of mine. Then a hand reaches down and my chest surges and she eases off her shoes, releasing a delicate, private bouquet. With a sigh the door opens, her fingers hooked to carry the shoes, lifting them out of my sight, and there is a glimpse of her bare feet—a flash of toenail (red! as expected!)—and then the door is shutting and the locks are locking—

And because she is barefoot I can't hear her walking away, she is instantly a ghost, ghosted, STILETTO soft now and shoeless and who knows when she is coming back. I whimper; my ankle is killing me. I need to pee. I could get out—I have to get out—I could stand outside her house, look through her windows, find her face. But I don't; I stay where I am, pleasureless, inhaling the cold sick smell of car carpet and my own damp crotch.

I ease my phone from the pocket of my coveralls and dial each of my brothers until one of them answers. I close my eyes and say I need a ride, and Carl makes a farting sound with his mouth and says Where are you? I imagine STILETTO's front door—I imagine knocking—I imagine her letting me in.

I'm here, I say, and then I hang up.

SHOP LADY

There's a woman, I don't know if you know her, she works downtown, she's a clerk at Kessler's jewelry store. Men come in and stare at the ropes of silver and gold she lays across her hands; they never know what to buy so they say What do you think? And she always recommends the middle-priced one, so they'll understand she isn't just trying to get more money, she honestly thinks this is the best one. They pull out their wallets and put them on the counter, they flip through a stack of cards and rub their foreheads. She wraps what she's chosen in tissue paper and a box with a shiny ribbon. That makes the men happy, they can barely remember on the way home what she has put inside, but they don't worry. It's always a hit, she has the touch, she knows what people are going to like. When it's slow and there are no husbands or groups of women whispering and looking at their phones the woman leans against the counter, she's tired, she has one foot wrapped around the ankle of the other as she rubs her tights together. Then someone comes in and she puts both heels on the floor; she smiles and runs her hand along the glass counter looking like she has just come out of a dream.

How I know all this is I'm watching her. When I moved here with my dad a few months ago I made friends with this girl, Charity, and we started to skip school and come down here almost every week to this coffee place across from where the jewelry shop is. When we sat on the curb to smoke I started noticing this woman in the shop. The store is almost all windows so you can see everything and after a while you get to know the kind of customers who go in and you know which one is shopping for his wife or girlfriend, which one is just looking, which one is bored or whatever and doesn't care how much something costs. The shop lady smiles at everyone, not in a fake way, but like she really cares about selling all this stuff. She has dark skin, maybe she's Spanish or Italian, and she wears long dresses and little quilted jackets and some of the jewelry they sell in the shop.

Today I'm downtown by myself because Char's grounded for ditching school. It's really hot and the place is crawling with tourists who act like they've never seen a palm tree before. This guy comes up to me, some old bum, and he's all Hey I'll give you a kiss if you give me a quarter. I tell him to fuck off, and he holds up his arms and says *Soorrrrry* and he laughs at me and I stub out my cigarette and start walking back to the coffee shop, wondering why the only people who talk to me are psychos or freaks.

I don't know when I started thinking about buying something at Kessler's but it just happened that every time I'd see the shop lady I'd think about doing it. The nicest place I'd ever been in was the Nordstrom's where Char and I looked for some underwear but there was too much security so we left. I don't even like jewelry that much, but I'm thinking about it a lot, just what it would be like to go in there and talk to her, to have her show me stuff and then say, Yes, I'd like that one, or No, I'd better not, not today. Finally I just take my dad's wallet while he's in the shower and think, Fuck it, why not, and go.

When I walk into Kessler's the shop lady starts looking at my ripped-up jeans, my hair. I dyed it and it came out kinda orange. But she just smiles at me like it doesn't matter. I sort of stand around like I don't know what I'm doing, which I don't, and she comes over to me and says Hello, can I help you with something?

I mess with my bangs and say My mom is really sick, I want to get her something for her birthday, something nice. The woman makes a sound like she's sorry about my mom and then she takes me over to some cases where some rings are stuck on velvet fingers.

I take my time, saying something about each one, how the color is nice or I like the way the metal is braided on that one, it looks really good. What price range are you looking at? she asks, and I say it doesn't matter, I'm not wanting to break the bank but it's a family gift for my mom so we want it to be special. She shows me a few rings, holding them with a cloth, and she smiles and waits like she has all the time in the world for me to make up my mind. Finally I say Well, it's between the purple and the ruby one, I just can't decide, and she says after a little pause You know for an older woman the ruby can be an overpowering stone, while the lighter stones, the amethysts, they really complement any skin tone and are appropriate for everyday wear. I say I hadn't thought of that, and then I say I want it, will she please wrap it up for me?

It's over $200 and when she runs the card through the machine I get a sick feeling in my stomach. But she doesn't even ask for ID. We make small talk as she wraps the ring and puts it into a glossy bag, just the right size for the ring box. I say thank you and she says she hopes my mother gets well soon. As I'm walking out one of those husbands comes in, he's got a giant bald spot and some nice suit on. Good luck, I say, and he gives me this look like he can't understand English but I keep smiling, I'm happy for the first time in a long time and when I get to the bus stop I unwrap the ring and put it in my pocket.

When I get home Dad is pissed; he's like Where's my wallet have you seen it? And I go, Uh no, where did you put it last, but he doesn't listen, it's obvious he's been freaking out for a few hours. I dropped his wallet in the trash, I felt bad but he hardly had any cash in it and anyway I only bought the one thing on the card, he can probably get it all back from the company when he says it was stolen.

When Char's mom ungrounds her we smoke in the park and then go downtown for coffee and Char catches me looking out the window. Why are you always looking over there? she asks and I shrug, playing with the straw in my drink. I don't know, I say, and suddenly she's not interested, she's grabbing my arm with her black nails digging into me saying OhmyGod did I fucking tell you about this shit that went down last night at Josh's? And I just stop listening.

The thing is, I know the shop lady. I know the different dresses she has, what kind of coat she wears when it's raining. I recognize her lipstick if another girl is wearing it, a kind of red brown like wet clay. When someone isn't in the store and she thinks no one is looking she lets her face get tired but as soon as someone walks in she smiles again and the great thing is that her face smiles too.

This is what I'm thinking when this guy comes in and Char's looking at me like *you like him?* His hair has blond streaks from being out in the sun and he keeps his thumbs hooked inside his jeans. He's a surfer and normally I hate surfers but he's kind of amazingly hot and I ask Char what she thinks and she shakes her head and says he's too white for her. I want a Mexican, she says, and laughs. Mexicans are fucking hot.

You are so racist, I tell her. The surfer guy gets a muffin and a coffee and he looks at Char and I spill my drink on purpose so it gets on Char's shorts and she screams What the fuck, Jessica! And the guy looks away and I can't help but laugh.

At one point I'm home and watching TV and I'm like Did you find your wallet? All bored and flipping through the channels and he says No, it's a real bitch having to cancel all the cards and get new ones and he keeps talking and I just go Uh-huh. Later when we're eating frozen burritos he asks me what's wrong because my face is all blotchy from crying and he seems like he really wants to know so I tell him that Char might be moving at the end of the year because her parents want her in a different school for people who are smart like her and it's really far away. Well she needs to focus on her education, Jessica, he says, trying to be all practical about it, and I stop eating and say Don't you get it she's my best *friend* and he goes Well if you tried you could make more friends instead of just moping around with that look on your face and your ass on the couch. What do you care, I say, and then he looks at me sort of funny and says I *do* care, and I don't say anything back, just eat another burrito.

After he puts the TV on and I know he won't hear me I put on my hoodie and leave out my window. I put the ring in my pocket and head downtown. It's a long walk but it's still light and Kessler's doesn't close until seven.

    I'm there when she gets off work. I've gone through

half a pack just waiting for her to get done cleaning up or whatever. When she walks out she has a big black coat on. Two security guards are with her and they look at me for a second but then say good night to her and start walking away. When she turns toward the parking lot I step in her path and say Hi, you don't remember me maybe but I got a ring here last week for my mom. I say You were right about the ring, it was just what she wanted. The shop lady looks startled but she smiles, that's how she is, she's polite. I'm glad, she says, and then we both just stand around, me chewing on my nails and her just looking like she doesn't know what to do. Finally I say Hey listen, do you think we could get a cup of coffee, it's really cold, I know a good place right there across the street, but the look on her face is all wrong and what I've said is stupid, I know, because it's like I'm asking her on a date when that's not what I mean at all. Well, it's really late, she says, I don't think so. And like some idiot I start crying and she's like What, what's wrong, but I can't say what, and now the woman is taking a step back, she has this expression like she's kind of sorry, but her sorriness is slipping and something else is taking its place. I'm sorry, she says, but I have to go, and then she makes as if to touch my shoulder and I, I don't know, I scratch her, on her wrist, scraping my nails against the bracelet she has on, some kind of gold cuff. Both our eyes go wide. She doesn't make a sound, she just turns and walks away really fast and I yell something after her, something like *You bitch*, which doesn't make any sense because she isn't a bitch, she isn't anything bad I could call her, she is the nicest person I know.

THE FIRE

She started out tiny, blue, a skinny flame flashing into the world with a hungry little sizzle. I gazed at her as she twisted between my thumb and forefinger, not knowing then what she would be like, if she would love me, or if I would love her—I didn't even know if she would be a she. That was left to fate. But right away I knew she would last. I could see it, how much she wanted it, as she strained toward the forest floor.

Leaping from my hand she shot through the parched undergrowth, becoming first a molten red line, then a skirt of orange, then rising, in an instant, into slender stalks of gold a foot high: gorgeous. She was a she, I thought, definitely.

Hello, John, she crackled, stroking me with her smoking fingers; I held out my hands and returned her caresses, delighted by the fine black skin she laid on top of my own sweating one.

Hungry? I asked.

Yes, she sighed, licking her way up the first tree.

There's plenty, I assured her. All for you.

Good, she whooshed, as the wind combed her eastward into the next dry crown of parched pine: Good good. Her heat sucked my eyes dry, toasted the hair on my head. Whispering encouragement I lay belly-down in the dirt, keeping as close to her as I could. *Enchanting!* I cried as she tossed her flames higher into the night sky. *Beautiful! Well done!* She had the wind, and she was strong; when I heard the first sirens advance, deep in the city below us, she had already grown far beyond my field of vision.

Darling, I gasped, ravished, grinning: Run.

The forest threw itself beneath her. That night she burned a thousand acres; the next night she took four times that number. She was relentless, voracious; she jumped fire lines like a girl skipping rope. The state, deep in a budget crisis, scrambled to rally its impoverished fire departments, but the predictions from the outset were dire; moving at fifteen miles an hour, burning at a thousand degrees, she was truly a wild thing.

Most of us in the valley could see her flames from our doorsteps, and everyone everywhere in the city could see her smoke rolling over the sky. I kept my windows open, hoping to catch her scent; I drew hearts in the ash she sprinkled on the sill.

John, she said, when you come tonight, bring me something.

Anything. What would you like?

Paper. Gas cans. Hairspray. Your clothes.

Which ones? I asked, already plunging my hands into my closet, my drawers.

All of them.

Only in the first forty-eight hours could I still reach her by one of the secret paths not cordoned off, paths only she and I knew, though even then I had to be careful not to be seen; I drove with my lights off, parked my van off the road. I carried the gifts, in boxes, a half mile up to where she was just beginning to flicker into new territory. By the time I reached her I was panting inside my fire mask, my arms strengthless, jellied with pain, but I didn't mind; it was worth anything to see her shimmering with delight over the boxes as I peeled back the flaps.

Paper? I offered.

Please, she snapped, and I fed a ream to her whole, watching as the pages were sucked high up into the air before flashing into flame. Next came the gas can, which

I hurled as hard as I could; it touched the edge of her and burst. I whooped, lobbing the hairspray cans like grenades. The clothes I spread out in a neat heart shape, jeans and T-shirts and underwear and socks and shoes all braided together, a baseball cap in the center.

These are for you, sweetheart, I said, and she rushed forward as I ran back, grasping the clothing in her eager fists. While she gobbled up my little tokens she was also plunging through the trees, and I pushed up the mask and put my forehead against the ground to feel how the earth shook beneath the tremendous boom and smack of exploding pine.

Yes! I yelled. My lips had split; blood crept from the dry flesh and I sucked it. She was kissing me. This was the taste of her. I jerked my hips in the dirt.

You are incredible, I said, her heat bearing down on my back. The forest floor was all ash, soft, hot: I thought I knew how it felt. I thought how lucky the forest was, to feel her so thoroughly, so deeply; it wanted her, it gave no resistance. It had been dry for so long. *You're welcome*, I told it.

I had a fox this morning, she confessed. And rabbits. Hundreds of rabbits. The birds drop down before I even touch them. They curdle in their nests.

I'm so glad, I said, inhaling the faint tang of scorched flesh and fur among the perfume of hot rock and charred wood. Such richness! She should have all of it and more, I thought; I wanted to drape her in meat and wood as a man might drape a woman in diamonds.

I lay there for as long as I dared, recklessly abandoning the mask for minutes at a time, gulping great lungfuls of smoke; when I coughed my saliva was black.

You're inside me already, I marveled.

Yes, John, she sighed. Isn't it nice?

I packed my van with my maps and a radio, a blanket, and a few cans of beans; she was on the move. For days I drove, my radio going nonstop with news of her direction, speed, appetite; I matched it mile for mile, working my way as close to her borders as was allowed. The relentless heat sucked the sweat from my skin; the driver's seat was constantly damp, as were the blankets I slept on in the rear. I tied a bandanna around my head, and no matter what I ate I tasted only ash and salt.

Though the emergency security cordons kept me at a distance she felt closer than ever, striking the landscape wherever I looked: she was 20,000 acres strong, then 50,000, then 100,000. She was the biggest, the most devastating news, raging behind every bewildered bleached-blond reporter, flaming the front pages of all the newspapers. There were a thousand firefighters struggling helplessly against her, eating up millions of tax dollars, unable to halt her astonishing progress.

Buckets of flame retardant were flown overhead and tipped along her back; I could hear her laughter as they struck her, harmless.

Look at you, I said, fanning the newspaper clippings across the floor of the van. The satellites can see you from space!

What's space? she asked.

It's everything around us that's not a thing.

She sighed. I want that, she said. I want all of it.

You'll have it, sweetheart, I assured her. It's already yours.

Yay, she said.

Yay, I echoed. I could feel her smiling, and I could see it, too, in the trees, at the very top, all mouth when she wanted to be, at other times all hands, or legs, dancing in the wind.

But as well as I knew her, as constantly as I tried to anticipate her needs and satisfy them, I did make the occasional mistake.

How's the woods this evening? I asked one night, early on in our relationship; we were in the habit of eating dinner together after I'd parked for the night, me in the front seat, her blazing off in the distance.

Delicious, she said. What are you having?

Egg salad, I told her. The gas-station sandwich was maybe a little spoiled from sitting on the dash all day, but I ate it anyway, then washed it down with the first thing at hand: old water from a half-gallon jug I'd found beneath the front seat.

What's that? she asked.

I paused, the water glugging in the jug. What's what?

That *sound*, she hissed.

I was just—drinking something.

Water?

Well—

Don't! she shrieked.

Sorry, sorry, I said, capping the jug and tossing it out the window, wincing when it hit a boulder.

Gosh, John, I mean, really!

I'm sorry. I'm stopping, I stopped. Okay? Honey?

There was only the sound of the tires on the road, the whip of passing cars. I glanced in my rearview mirror, but saw only smoke, no flame.

Hey, I said. Talk to me.

I'm busy.

Busy what?

Burning!

Of course, I said. I'm sorry.

Another silence, and then: Turn on the radio, she gusted gently. We gasped with pleasure when we heard the chorus of our favorite song, "Burning Down the House." We sung in unison, as loud as we could, her voice and my voice in perfect harmony inside the cab of the old van.

She was, indeed, busy: at five weeks and 500,000 acres she was busier and busier. Hundreds were evacuated from threatened homes, and though she hadn't yet taken a neighborhood, she longed for one, bidding me time and again to describe what was in store: glass, garages, tennis courts, palm trees, pools. She had already had a few stray cars. *Tires*, she enthused. *Oh, John, the tires!*

I kept driving, drinking Gatorade and eating bags of peanuts, soaking up the news. We had a lot to be proud of: she was on the cover of several local and national magazines, appeared on countless television shows, broke wildfire records daily. She grinned into the eyes of a hundred cameras, a thousand cell phones; I had a folder full of photos downloaded from libraries, her flames captured from every angle. Everyone for a hundred miles knew the name the papers gave her, but only I knew her true name, which was not a word but both a sound and a sight, a tremendous lightning roar scrawling itself across the parched earth.

In the evenings I would park the van and walk along the hills, as close as I could get to her, just off the freeway, the wind whipping my reeking T-shirt as we talked. There had never been anything like this in my life, nothing to prepare me for the intensity of my love for her, my happiness, my admiration, though there had been, I confessed, others: a half-dozen attempts in dry fields when I was a boy, a few Dumpster fires. Later, in my twenties and thirties, there'd been more serious encounters: a saucy little house blaze in the suburbs, an all-night conflagration at an abandoned lumber mill, the short-lived but brilliant rager at a used-furniture shop in the suburbs.

Did you love them?

No, I assured her, never. They were brave girls, all of them, and beautiful, yes, but they could not compare. Loving her was like loving a queen, or a mountain; she dominated me, she made me a subject, and yet when I looked into the van's mirrors I didn't see a plain soot-stained face or matted hair or a body encased in filthy rags; I saw something purer, lighter. I was untethering myself from the world of flesh. I was slowly becoming free.

Of course, I was not the only one in her thrall. Other admirers flocked by the dozens to the scenic-view pull-outs off the highway: middle-aged men with canvas hats flapping in the high hot wind, teenagers in muscle T-shirts and cutoffs, vagabonds driving dusty RVs; young foreign couples with slick lips and beautiful hair. They carried binoculars, bag lunches, digital cameras,

lattes and iced teas and Slurpees, expensive phones, cigarettes. I sat on the hood of my van, and though they
took turns staring, no one spoke to me, and I had no
desire to speak to them.

I don't understand why they don't have more men
on the ground, a woman complained, flipping a gray
braid over her shoulder. It's only twenty miles from the
housing complex.

Who cares about some rich people's houses, a young
man replied, scowling, his matchstick arms sleeved
from wrist to bicep in ink. It's nature's revenge, man.
Humans are parasites.

You include yourself in that statement? the woman
scoffed.

Hell yes, I do.

State's spending as much as they can. It's a reces-
sion, someone added.

You can't just let people's property burn! the woman
insisted. Someone shushed her and she turned, catching
my eye, and scowled at me, though I had said nothing.
There was a huge boom from the fire; a balloon of fresh
flame splattered the sky. Everyone flinched and the boy
laughed, a high, hysterical sound.

I heard it was man-made, a Japanese woman said,
looking at her phone. They think it was started in the
Valley by a homeless person.

Other voices chimed in: Probably some idiot burning trash.

Nah, they would have found something at the origin site. It's arson.

I heard some guy already turned himself in but they're keeping his name a secret.

If I knew that bastard's name I'd hang him myself. Me and my kids are sleeping on my mother's living-room floor because of this goddamn evacuation.

Freaks get off on it, someone grumbled.

You'd have to be sick in the head to even think about it. Forget about property, it's people's *lives* at stake.

Why do you people always have to blame shit on someone? the tattooed boy said. There's been, like, a *drought*. Fires happen, man. Accept it. It's not about you and your stupid *house*.

The braid lady glared at the boy. He raised his fist and flipped her off.

Another woman was fitting a camera with a lens; as she raised it to her eye the darkly bearded man next to her said She's really something, isn't she.

My head whipped toward him. How did he know she was a she? He was smiling, nodding to himself, looking now and then through a huge pair of binoculars, nicer than the ones I had in my van.

As the evening passed into true night the others

climbed back into their cars, but this man stayed, a half hour, an hour. I was sitting on a rock, jiggling my knees, moving only to pee behind my van; when I came back around, he was still there. The traffic had thinned at our backs and the only light came from the moonlight trapped in the smog.

Getting late, I said, loud. No answer. I peered at him; there was something funny about his expression, his eyes fixed so relentlessly through the enormous binoculars, his lips curving into a little private smile I could almost feel on my own face.

It's really late to be out, isn't it? I repeated. For a moment I thought I could see his mouth moving, like he was talking, but I couldn't hear any sound.

What? I said.

He didn't even look in my direction.

Hey, I shouted, leaping up from the rock, gravel spitting beneath my shoes. Hey! Knock it off!

He did a double take, trying to dodge the finger I was thrusting in his face.

Excuse me?

Don't you dare talk to her! Don't you even *look* at her!

He swatted at my arm. Who?

Her! Her! I screamed.

I don't know what—

You fucking bastard! I shrieked, throwing myself at his chest; then we were both on the ground, grappling, feet sliding over the blacktop. I jabbed my elbow into his stomach, but the angle wasn't right and I don't think he even felt it.

Are you out of your goddamn mind? he spat, chopping at my head with his big hands; I managed to grab a fistful of his hair before a blow to the temple folded me sideways. I threw my leg out as I fell off him, crushing my heel into the meat of his thigh.

Jesus! he yelled, heaving himself from the ground. Limping he backed his way to the hood of his car, half bent, his eyes wide on my face.

You—how do you—how dare—I sputtered, rolling to my side.

Don't get up! I'll call the cops! he said.

I lifted my head, seeing pink.

I heard the door of his Jeep slam shut; the engine roared. Gravel and dirt peppered my jeans as he peeled into the road.

You'll burn! I shouted. *I'll burn you up!*

Nutjob! he called through the window. I watched his taillights rake red through the dark, then disappear.

I sat up. I'm bleeding, I told her, touching the split skin above my eye.

Oh, poor John, she said.

It'll be okay, I replied, pressing the hem of my shirt to the wound. Did you know that guy?

She paused. Well, in a way.

What way?

He's around, here and there.

I took the shirt away from the wound, rubbed my thumb in the circle of blood. Where?

Other sites. He comes every day, almost.

What?

He knows an awful lot about fires, she added.

I don't *believe* this! I shouted, kicking one of the van's tires as hard as I could.

Stop yelling, she said, suddenly stern. She'd already knocked two dozen firemen unconscious that afternoon; she wasn't going to take any crap from me. I slapped a gnat on the back of my neck, panting.

I'm not yelling.

Yes, you are.

Sorry, I mumbled.

I don't *talk* to him, silly. I don't talk to anyone but you, she whooshed, the wind bringing some smoke straight into my face. I took a deep breath, coughed, smiled.

Well, good, I said, pulling myself inside the van. My torso hurt, the side of my right leg hurt, my face hurt. I was thirsty from sitting outside all day with only the cold half cup of someone's Starbucks to drink. But it didn't matter; the guy was gone, and we were alone. I rummaged in the glove compartment and found a sleeve of melted Thin Mints and ate a few, lying in the back of the van, my head heavy on the greasy pillow, the side door cracked open on a slice of undulating flame. The whole van, everything I touched, smelled like her, felt like her: sharp and dry and hot.

He's right, you know, I murmured.

Who?

That guy. You are really something.

Oh, John, she replied, cradling me in her many arms—heat, ash, smoke, roar, light—until I slipped into sleep.

And then we lost the wind.

It came as a surprise, even to the weather people, who had predicted strong air currents for the next week. *No*, I said when I woke up and saw how still the trees were, how motionless the scrub brush and dust along the roads. Her flames rose straight up and down, like people standing around at a party, no longer like sprint runners slicing through the hills.

Shit, I said, shit shit shit!

Where is it? John, where did it go? she demanded.

I don't know, I said, slapping at the radio, trying to

get some good news. There was none. I slammed the steering wheel with my fist, sending the van careening into the left-hand lane. I could feel her heat inside the car, thick with panic; it made me breathless.

I pulled over at the next turnout, parked, rolled down my windows. It's a temporary setback, I said, forcing myself to be calm. Think of it as a little break. You can focus on getting really hot on the northern front, get everything nice and dry, and when the wind picks up again, *boom!* You'll gain whatever ground they'll take in a day. All right?

All right, she said, I'll try.

She wanted to believe me, and I couldn't believe anything else. But the state saw its chance; more men were sent, from Oregon, from Arizona, from New Mexico. Three thousand reserves. Helicopters hovered nonstop, dumping their buckets. She could feel the fire-fighters coming closer, she said, she could hear their footsteps on the ground. They were approaching from the east, the south; they were attacking from behind, from the side, mopping up what had already burned, blasting her weakest points in hopes of thinning her out while the wind was down. *North! North!* I yelled over the sound of the radio, huddled over the maps and a calculator in the back of the van. But to the north there were only a few hundred acres of forest before she would meet mountains; she could not climb them. And west was where she had already been. Suddenly the world, which had seemed so large when I met her, had shrunk to nothing, nowhere.

Those were dark, sleepless days. I lived off caffeine pills, camped in the van, refusing to go anywhere for anything—no food, no Gatorade, nothing. I did not recognize her voice, screaming in a new language of pain and rage as blankets of water and retardant snuffed her out an acre at a time. She could barely move, and beneath the swollen cloud of her own smoke she was choking.

On the radio the chief of operations triumphantly reported their gains on the blaze. The news poured bleaker and bleaker from the radio; finally it became so horrible I ripped the batteries from the plastic case, shoved the maps beneath the seats. I dropped from the side of the van onto the tarmac and looked at the sky to see if what I'd heard was true.

Behind me, coming from the south, crept a blanket of low gray cloud.

Sweetheart, listen, I said.

What? she asked. What now?

I took a deep breath. They're saying it's going to rain.

Rain? How much?

I don't know. It could be a lot, I whispered.

She thought for a moment, and I could feel it, her

thinking, the way her mind reached through the tips of her, feeling the sky for information.

A few days, she decided. At most.

They could be wrong, I said, black snot trembling on my lip. They've been wrong before.

No, John, she said, and her voice now was quiet, firm. There was nothing we could do to help each other. All we could do was wait for it to begin.

Ribs of white light cracked through the sky and we screamed. The clouds gushed; she sizzled like raw flesh slapped on a grill. A fire truck drove past on the road behind me, its sirens quiet, gloating. You fucking murdering fuckheads, I whispered, chin to my chest, my legs giving way. You *bas*tards.

It was the sixty-seventh day of her burning; I'd been awake for forty-eight hours, lying on my side on the ground somewhere in the foothills, the rain slashing through the soot on my skin. She blinked at me from the husks of trees, embers like eyes, a million of them, blinking, blinking, before going dark.

It's so cold, John, she hissed, so faint I could barely hear her. I'm so cold.

The next night a small, hushed group gathered at the lookout, umbrellas open, hoods up and dripping. I was slumped on the other side of the guardrail, my back pressed against the cool metal. The fresh air slicing through the haze was hateful to me, as was the smell of coffee from the cups the others clutched; but even they could see how terrible it was. We stood like pilgrims beholding the body of a dragon, sober-faced; for a long time no one spoke. We watched the glitter of water falling in slow stabs from the sky. The hills were fireless as far as the eye could see.

Finally a child asked Is it over?

Yes, its father answered.

Thank God, someone else added. Then silence again. I held my head in my hands. I was dry inside, so dry I could burn. And I am burning still.

FUGUE

The girl works nights. In the middle of nowhere. She drives an hour to get to her job, an hour back. She can stand through her entire shift in silence, the way she is standing now. Dim white light spills down over her. The dessert freezer builds up ice. She is allowed to help herself to some chips or beef jerky or a cold drink. She likes how quiet it is, how dark it is. It is the quiet that brought her here.

The boys are driving in the young one's black car. They know all about girls like her, girls who are alone, girls not beautiful, but not unattractive, either. In her uniform like a mechanic, blue, no name tag: hair like thick silk. No makeup.

Did you know testosterone is just, like, a drug? the tall one says.

Major drug, the youngest one says.

Turn the music down, the dark-haired one says. I can't hear anything.

Shut your mouth, the young one replies, and turns the music up.

The storefront is humped concrete and plate glass; they can see the girl from the road, her ponytail in the window.

Hey, the tall one says, slapping the young one's arm. Get off here.

What? the young one says, focused on a smear of road kill just beyond the steering wheel.

Don't we need gas? the tall one asks, and when he points they all look.

Fuck yeah, the young one says, and pulls the car around. Three slow smiles stretch inside the car.

They pull in alongside the gas pumps. One of the overhead lamps is broken. They get out of the car in slow motion, like gangsters in a movie; in their heads music is playing. They hitch up their pants and push into the store. The air inside is cool, stale. They run their hands over everything: rows of gummy bears in plastic bags on pegboard, canned nuts settling in drifts of salt, bags of chips sagging on the shelves. In the beverage cases the energy drinks wink neon, lined two or three deep; cold shadows yawn behind them. The tall one spins a rack of maps and a postcard spills out of a broken pocket: *Wish you were here!* He kicks it under the ice cream freezer.

The girl watches them from behind the register, crowned by slots of cigarettes, her palms on the counter. The boys advance from different aisles; the youngest gets to her first, then the tall one. The dark-haired one, whose eyes are also dark, almost black, is last, his thumbnail raking across the face of the magazine display as he approaches.

Hey, the young one says, leaning over the counter, hip cocked.

Hi, the girl replies. She looks at each of them, in order, left to right. You need some gas? she asks.

Maybe, the young one says.

The dark-haired one slides a lotto ticket out of a stack near the girl's fingers; digging a dime from his pocket he scratches the card, his tongue between his teeth. Beneath the silver foil he finds four clovers.

Shit, he says, rearing back with pleasure. What'd I win?

The girl reads the fine print. A dollar, she says.

The other boys laugh. She punches a button on the register; the drawer jumps open and the tall one leans to look inside.

How much you got in there?

I don't know, she says. A few hundred, I guess. She talks slow, kind of quiet, but not shy; she looks them in the eyes and smiles.

What if we made you give it to us?

She blows on her bangs. You got a gun?

Maybe.

Then I guess I'd have to give it to you.

The tall one slips a dollar from the tray.

Nah, he says. But we won this fair enough, right? Snapping the bill in her face.

She flinches, giggling. He puts the bill in the take-a-penny-leave-a-penny tray.

You should get a tip jar, he says.

For real, the young one says. The tall one sucks his lips.

You smoke?

Sure, she replies.

You wanna smoke with us? It's good shit, the dark-haired one says, his hips caressing the front of the counter. We promise.

Sounds great, she says, and if the boys were listening they could hear it—the wall clock telling them it is

time to keep driving. But they aren't listening. The blood
roars in their ears.

I know a good place to do it, she says.

You've done this before? the tall one asks.

Sure, she says. Haven't you?

The young one puts his hand next to hers, his pin-
kie dancing over the side of her palm. He looks at the
others like, see? Easy.

Outside, moths swarm in flammable mass against the
store windows. The empty parking lot glitters, a sea of
spilled tar, and they cross it into the short strip of damp
grass bordering the lot and the road. Dew licks their
shoes; the tall boy dips his head to smoke but the young
one puts his hand over the cigarette, folds it in his
palm, drops it. The girl is in front, head down, ponytail
swinging, as they walk beneath the concrete horizon of
the overpass, where no cars move. The young one smiles
and the tall one smiles, too; the dark-haired one lifts his
shoulders inside his track jacket, cold from the inside.

Beneath the pass the girl stops. They're standing in a
stretch of soft dirt and stone hooded by the road: beyond the girl the boys can't see anything but the dim
skeleton of a chain-link fence. The girl faces the boys,
and the young one rubs his toe in the dirt.

———————

So is it good? she asks.

Is what good?

She blinks. Your trip, she says. You're on a road trip, right?

The young one chuffs. We're just driving.

Oh, she says. Cool.

What's your name? the tall one asks. The girl cocks her head, small smile buzzing around her lips.

What's yours? she replies.

You want us to guess? the dark-haired one asks, but the young one snorts, shakes his head.

We're not playing games, man. She doesn't want to say, then she doesn't want to say.

Laura, the tall one says. She looks like a Laura.

The girl looks at him. What does a Laura look like?

Like you.

Is that good?

The tall one shrugs. It's not bad, he says.

Are we just going to stand here or what, the dark-haired one says, pushing his fists in his jacket.

The young one pulls a joint out of his pocket and dances it in front of the girl. She reaches for it, but he lifts it away from her hand, whistling.

I thought we weren't playing games, the girl says.

Maybe we are, maybe we aren't, the young one says. You don't have anything better to do, do you?

No, she agrees.

Then relax. Open your mouth, he says, and the girl parts her thin lips. He sets the end of the joint next to her tongue.

The lighter's in my back pocket, the young one says, looking down at her pale face.

The girl reaches around the young one's waist. Her eyelid flutters when her hand bumps something cool and hard. She pulls it out.

Try again, the tall one says, taking the Swiss army knife from the girl and, peeling the scissors from the steel grip, starts cutting his nails.

The girl's smile deepens. She reaches into the young one's other pocket.

Here? she says.

You got it, he says, then plucks the joint from her mouth. But how about a kiss first?

She tilts her head up, her lips still parted.

You want to fuck? she whispers, before he can kiss her, and for a moment the boys are frozen.

Hey now, the young one says, giving the girl his smooth laugh. He grinds the lighter, flipping on its weak fire: smell of burning, of a good time. The young one takes a deep breath. The girl licks her lips.

The dark-haired one sees it happen first: the emergence of the girl's real face. Her eyes seem to blacken; her mouth discards the dull smile. She is no Laura, it occurs to him; she is not an Allison or a Sarah or a Tiffany. There is no way this girl has a name like any name they know.

Hey—the dark-haired one says, trying to get the attention of the others, but they are still playing with the joint and their own anticipation; the dark-haired one might as well be a tree or a block of night sky.

The young one exhales into the girl's open mouth. That what you want? he says.

Ooh, she croons, running her finger down the young one's chest. You're gonna do it to me, I know it.

Their smiles flicker, fade. The girl turns to snatch the knife out of the tall one's half-clipped hands.

You wanna screw me with this?

What the fuck, the young one breathes, dropping the joint. He takes a step back.

You, she says. You can choke me. That will feel good, won't it? If you do that?

We're not into that shit, he says, wincing, hands up.

It's okay, she continues, pulling each tool from the red case, one by one. You can do it. I *like* it.

The tall one reaches for his knife but she whips it high above their heads, its splayed tools twinkling.

Maybe you should calm down, the dark-haired one says.

The girl sharpens her gaze on him.

You can watch, she says. And then you can have your turn.

What the fuck is wrong with you? the young one says.

Nothing, she says, blinking, eyes wider and wider. What's wrong with *you*? Why isn't your cock hard?

She nudges her knee against the inside of the young one's thigh; he jerks away.

This better be a joke, he says.

Why? she says. You feel like laughing?

Seriously, *what* the *fuck* is your *deal*?

Don't you like me? I thought you liked me, the girl says, pouting. She moves her head from side to side, like a leaking balloon, lips pushed out, making the high-pitched whimper of a dog. The knife lands in the dirt; no one moves to touch it. Her shoulders start to shake and her frown melts down and she pretends to cry, *boo-hoo*, cartoon sobs slashing out between her teeth. Every hair on every piece of the boys' skin stands up.

Let's just go, the tall one says, but nobody moves.

You can't go, you haven't done it yet, the girl says.

Fuck man let's just get—

The girl slaps herself, hard, so that her lip smashes against her teeth; blood darts down her chin. She staggers to the side.

No, she whispers.

The boys are stuck. The night is something that con-geals around them, in them, between them. They don't know how to move. She starts to undress: shoes, socks, polo, pants. The boys stare. The clothes lie like shed snake-skin at her feet. A jagged line runs from her navel down into the lip of her underwear, and from what they can see of her breasts those, too, are shiny with scars.

Fuck, the young one whispers.

You want to touch me? the girl asks.

We don't want to do anything, the tall one says.

Oh no? Then who did this? Do you know who did this? she says, jabbing at the scar on her belly.

No, the boys say.

You did it, the girl hisses. Don't you remember?

We should call someone, get someone, the cops— the dark-haired one says.

Who? she says, eyes narrowing. Call who? Then she laughs, a high bright sound punching the air.

Oh you bad boys, she says, her teeth pink. Such *bad* boys. Do you need your knife back? Is that why you haven't done it yet?

She kicks the ground, making the knife jump.

Done what?

Killed me! the girl shrieks.

You're crazy, the young one breathes.

The girl cocks her head, smiling hard. The dark-haired one puts his hands up to his head.

I don't know what's going on, he says. I don't know why we don't *go*.

Oh, you can do whatever you want, she says. There are three of you and one of me. Isn't that fair?

The boys open their mouths but the words that fall out lie in the dirt and never seem to reach the girl. In time they grow silent; they grow still as trees.

Do you know how many times there isn't anyone? she says at last. No one at all? Once, I counted just six cars. Six. In eight hours. And none of them stopped, even though I was screaming as loud as I could.

JAILBAIT

For stealing two beers and giving a clerk the bird at a Super Stop I spend one night in jail. They put me in a cell with eight other guys waiting for their rides. I ask someone lying on the only bench if I can sit down. The guy stretches out his legs and tells me to fuck off.

I get my one phone call and talk to Bea at a pay-phone-type situation chained to the wall. It's five in the morning and neither of us has slept; I'm smiling into the receiver and I can tell she's smiling, too.

I came right then, she tells me, her voice so warm and close I know she's got her mouth right up against the phone. Just, God, the back of your head, she says. When they put the cuffs on you and made you get in the car. It was the hottest thing I've ever seen in my life.

Within a week Bea's asking me if I'll do it again. I do, same store, same beer. The clerk is making the call before I can get the cans in my jacket pockets. The cops ask me what the hell I'm doing. I say I'm thirsty. I think about Bea, in the parking lot, watching me. I get a hard-on and I hope she can see it, though maybe it's too dark. In the backseat I ask the cops if they can turn on the siren and they say, Shut up, wiseass.

This time, when they book me, I'm in a holding cell by myself, but only for a few hours before the cops tell me to stop wasting their time.

Bea comes to get me, hyper, eyes jumping like she's coked up. Just being near the jail gets her this way. She tries to look past the lobby to where the cells are, but a set of green double doors blocks her view.

What happened? she asks. Did anything happen?

Not really, I say.

Why are they letting you out so soon?

I guess they need the room, I reply, shrugging. They don't think stealing beer is a big deal.

Bea's mouth goes hard. You need to do something bigger, like a car, she tells me.

How?

It doesn't matter. Smash the window or something.

I tell her that auto theft is a lot more serious than filling my pockets at the Super Stop.

That's the point, idiot, she says.

I say You're crazy, and then she's mad, and we drive the rest of the way in silence.

At home she darts out of reach whenever I put my hands out to touch her. Come on, I groan; she shakes her head, stomping around the coffee table, rummaging for cigarettes, the remote, casting me these little pissed-off glances. When I try to talk about something else she turns the TV up louder and louder.

Okay! I say finally. Okay, I'll do it, shit, and she yelps and throws her arms around my neck, practically choking me.

Tomorrow, she says. Do it tomorrow.

And that's how I end up with a tire iron in my hand, crouched over the windshield of a red Mustang convertible. The glass spills like kid's cereal over the pavement and the car alarm goes nuts and the lights flip on in someone's house and I start running. The cops catch up with me about eight blocks away as I'm trying to hop a fence. Everyone's shouting and there are flashlights and radios and they tell me, just like in the movies, to put my hands up. They bend me over the squad car to cuff me, someone's hand on the back of my neck, while the cop radio makes noise.

What the fuck were you gonna do with this, asshole?

one of them says, holding the gun Bea told me to stick in my jeans, and I just laugh. I roll my face into the hood with my mouth open against the white paint so I can tell her later what it tastes like.

I get used to prison pretty fast. We have TV and a gym, and we don't all have to shower at the same time or anything. No one I talk to is a murderer or a rapist; mostly they're all just thieves or drug addicts and we play cards and talk about our girlfriends and that's it. Sometimes there's a fight or someone pisses on the floor but the prison guards are mellow and you know exactly what to expect out of your day.

At night I write letters to Bea. Five sheets per envelope per week, and I write as small as I can. I tell her how dangerous it is, how hard I'm getting fucked, how because I'm the skinniest guy in here I'm automatically the pussy. I tell her they make me shave my balls, that they choke me, that they come in my mouth and I have to swallow or else they'll beat the shit out of me. And I tell her that I like it, that even though it hurts and I'm afraid of them, I want it. I tell her I get hard and I come and they beat me for that, too. I tell her that no one uses condoms and I could get a terrible disease, I could die in here and no one would stop it from happening. She writes back and tells me what to say, how to act, how to let guys know they can use me. She signs every letter with a string of *x*'s and *o*'s half a page long and I put them over my face, imagining I can smell her hands, the Candy Apple lotion that I like so much, before tucking the pages beneath my pillow.

Which one do you share with? she asks during our first visiting hour. She looks incredible, in a short black dress with little red flowers on it and her hair puffed way out.

I jerk my head in the direction of the biggest man, black and bald, with arms like fire hydrants, talking to a woman who looks like his mom. Leaning way back in her chair Bea checks him out, eyes narrowed, and when the chair tilts forward again she's grinning.

What's his name?

Leroy, I say.

What's his prison name?

Big, um, Big—Big Daddy.

He wants to pretend he's your dad?

No, it's more like, he just wants to be in charge, you know?

How big? she asks. How big is it?

I hesitate, pretending like I don't want to say.

Just show with your hands, she urges, and I draw a slow line on the table, nine, ten inches long. Her eyes get huge.

No fucking way, she breathes. How much around? she asks.

I tap my lip, considering.

Like, I don't know. A—a soda can? I say, making a motion like I'm sipping from a Coke.

Oh my *God*, she says, slapping the table with her palms. What do they call you when they do it?

I told you already.

I know, but I want to hear you say it, she pleads.

Pussy, I whisper, my hand cupped against the side of my head to keep people from seeing the shape my mouth makes. She scrunches up her shoulders like a kid being tickled.

You're *so* the pussy, she says. I can tell by the way they look at you.

I'm pretty sure no one is looking at me, but I nod like I know what she means.

I love seeing you like this, she says. But wouldn't it be better, I mean, I always imagined it, like, through those big Plexiglas windows? With the phones?

I think that's for the big-time guys, felons and stuff, I say.

Huh, she says, and sucks her tooth the way she does when she's thinking hard about something.

We keep talking and the time flies by. I hold her hand until one of the guards tells me to stop.

It's not your fault, you know, she says. That you want this. That you need it.

No?

No, baby, she croons. You can't help it, and that's okay.

Okay, I say, and all of a sudden I'm not sure if I should smile, because I am smiling, a little, but she's looking at me like, no.

You're not too lonely? I ask her. She seems confused.

Oh God, she says. Are you kidding me?

When I get out she wants to see my ass, right there in the car, before we've even left the parking lot. I unbuckle my pants, slide them off my hips, and she folds herself between my legs, scrunched in the space below my seat, and squints like she's trying to read the directions on a box of instant potatoes. Without warning she spits and shoves two fingers inside me. I wince.

What the fuck, didn't they loosen you up at all? I thought you needed stitches, she grunts, working her fingers up to the knuckle.

It healed, I say, gasping. I want to look at her face but she won't let me; she tells me to keep my eyes on the window in case anyone sees us.

Why aren't you coming, she says, all out of breath.

I don't—if you could just slow down, maybe—

Slow down? You want me to slow down? Like hell you want me to slow the fuck down.

I—

You need cock, is that it? she says, and she is ecstatic when I say Yes, she jerks me off and kisses me so hard I can feel her teeth.

Baby, she says, over and over, Oh baby baby baby.

We stop and get sandwiches at a deli. Bea keeps looking at me, not smiling, more like she's studying me or something. When my knees touch hers under the table she moves them away.

You smell good, I say, and she blinks.

What? she says. What did you say to me?

Your perfume, I say.

I'm not wearing perfume, you jackass, she says.

I guess it's just been so long since I smelled a woman, like, up close, I tell her.

You don't want a woman anymore, she says, sucking on a Funyun. You don't want to smell a woman. You want to smell your own shit on a guy's cock, don't you?

Bea, I say, do you think we could just talk to each other for a moment? Talk about something else?

Why? 'Cause you want to feel normal? You're not normal. You're a fucking whore. You let all those guys fuck you and you liked it. I don't know what else there is to talk about.

I sip my Sprite. I want to tell her I missed her so

much, but instead I tell her she's right. I say You're right, and she finally smiles.

I know I am, she says.

The apartment is messier than I remember. The stove is crusted black, and all the dishes are stacked in the sink. The trash is crammed with boxes from microwave dinners and fast food. The whole place smells like sour milk. Above the mattress she's taped the picture she took of me in my prison uniform; the only part of my head that's showing is my chin, but you can tell that I'm smiling.

I take a shower while she watches me from the toilet, her knees pressed together and her feet arched up. The shower curtain is open and water bounces off my body and onto the floor.

Did they ever use anything other than their cocks? she wants to know.

The janitor used a broomstick, I say. And once Mikey used the handle of a razor.

Mikey? she says. Who's Mikey?

Mikey's the, uh, the new guy.

She slips her underwear down to her ankles and touches herself. I want to watch her but she says no, she wants me to put my hands on the tile and tell her how it was. I can hear how wet she is. Leaning my head against the tile I close my eyes. I tell her that Mikey is fucking me with the handle of the razor and I want to scream but he threatens to beat my head in if I so much as blink. He gets it all the way in and the blood running down my thighs is hotter than the hot water from the showerhead. The guards watch, the other guys watch, one of them is going to have a turn next, they talk about it, what they're going to do to my ass, and I'm so scared I piss myself, and that gets them all even more excited.

You wanted it and they knew it, Bea says.

Yes.

It was me doing it to you the whole time, she says. I want it to be me doing it to you.

Yes, I whisper, and she does that thing with her breathing, like she's crying, but it means she's coming.

Oh fuck, I love you, Jonathan, she says.

I love you too, I say.

Bea cleans houses some days but other days she seems to have nothing to do. I know there are bills she hasn't paid, that her mother is sending her money, and twice we wake up with no lights. She says that we're fine, and she's the one with the bank account so I don't say much about it. We watch TV, drink beer on the porch, sleep in the afternoon when it's hot so we can be awake at night when it's cool and the mosquitoes are gone.

Do you miss it? she asks.

No, I think. Yes, I say, putting my hand in hers.

I'm glad I'm home, though, I say. She touches my hair.

That's sweet, she says. But I know it can never really be home again.

I don't ask her what she means.

She says I can fuck her if I want, from behind. She leans over the kitchen sink, she tells me to pull her hair and I do it, she wants me to say I'm going to hurt her and I do that, too. She laughs when I come, a crazy laugh like she's drunk or high, and even though I want to be nice to her what I want more is to make her happy. So I put my arm around her neck and squeeze. She says Don't stop.

But it doesn't last. We go out, and it's a bad night. Our tacos don't taste right and the margaritas are watery and no matter what I say she doesn't look up from her food. I ask her if she wants to dance and she goes to the dance floor but she barely moves, and when I put my hands on her waist I can feel how tense her muscles are, like her whole body is a fist. She twists away, adjusting her tube top, and we drive home without saying anything.

On the porch when we're having a cigarette I ask her what's wrong, to please tell me, because I thought things were going so good. At first she shrugs, making a face like she doesn't want to talk, but I can tell that all along she's been wanting to say what she finally says.

It's nothing, she starts, sighing and scratching her cheek. It's just . . . it's not working.

What's not?

This, she says, gesturing between us. With you out. On the outside.

Sure it is, I say, reaching for her thigh.

No, she insists, inhaling sharply on her cigarette, shaking her head. It's not good like this. It's not what you need.

Yes, it is. It's exactly what I want.

Her head doesn't stop shaking.

Bea, it's what I want, everything's great.

No, she says again. You're not satisfied. I can't do it like you need it.

What? Yes—

No, Jonathan, fuck. Listen to me. She turns to face me, her earrings swinging against her chin. You have to go back.

I look at her with my mouth open.

Bea, I can't. If I do something again, it will be real time, like—

But that's the *point*, she says, getting so excited her butt lifts off the porch step, her hands a shaking pair of claws gripping an invisible ball. You need to do it for *real. Fuck* probation, *fuck* community service, you know? I want us to have a relationship, Jonathan, a real fuck- ing relationship, not just us fucking living here and drinking beer and living like every other fucking ass-hole in this fucking city!

Wait, slow down, Bea, what—

I try to catch one of her hands, but she only lets me touch her fingers for a moment before she's reaching for another cigarette.

Why don't you trust me? Why can't you admit what you really want?

I do, of course I do. I'm telling you what I really want and it's not those guys, for fuck's sake, that's not what it's about at all—

She laughs this mean little laugh as her thumb trips along her lighter.

Oh, it's not? Then what's it about, macho man?

I look at her and I don't know what she's thinking. I feel like I'm playing a game of Monopoly and she's got all the good property and no matter what I roll I'm going to owe her some big bucks.

It's just about—having fun, right? I say. Playing a game, right?

Fun? she spits, scrunching up her face.

Just for—like, because it's not real.

What?

It's not real? I say again, but as a question.

What's not real?

I pause, blinking.

It—the whole—the sex part? I stutter.

Jonathan, what the shit are you saying?

We made it up, right? Together, like . . . isn't that . . . what we did?

You made it up, she repeats, her voice flat, and I can see her nostrils quiver and the veins in her neck pulse hard and blue. She stares at me with eyes so wide I can see the whites all around the green part. For a long time we're just looking at each other.

You stupid fucking asshole, she says, her chin shaking, her lips pulled down. How dare you, she says, stubbing her cigarette out on the porch step. How fucking dare you.

And instead of yelling or screaming or hitting me, she cries. The tears just run down her face and she sniffs, standing up, and goes into the house and slams the door. I yell, I beg, but she doesn't let me in.

Finally I fall asleep on the porch. In the morning she drops a cardboard box of my clothes next to my head.

If you're here when I get back, she says, I'll kill you, and she stomps down the steps, sunglasses on and her hair uncombed, and she gets in our car and drives away.

She changes her phone number almost immediately. I think, Okay, give her a few days, let her calm down. When I get up the nerve to walk by the apartment someone else is there. I pound on the door, but the man who opens it says he's never heard of Bea, even though I can see all our furniture still inside. He says if I don't get the fuck off his porch he's going to call the cops.

I'm thinking of her face behind the glass in a real prison, her hand up to touch mine. I'm thinking of her smile, spread wide enough to show the molar with the dead nerve inside that turned the tooth gray.

Did you hear what I said, fuckface? the guy says, stepping into me.

I just stand there on the porch—my porch, me and Bea's porch—looking this guy in the face. I'll do whatever I have to do. And when the first man puts his hands on me, I'll be ready.

WHOLE LIFE AHEAD

'm so cold, she says, the first thing, her voice small and faraway, and he doesn't know if she is saying it to him or if it is something she has been saying for a long time before he got here. He clears his throat, says her name; she turns her head sharply, like a deer, on the edge of fright.

Hello? she says.

It's me, he tells her, and puts his hands on her arms. When she moves dirt falls on her shoulders, skips down her dress. He's aware that her back is only bones beneath the dress, skin shrunk against them like leather, but he doesn't mind; he expected worse.

Do you know how long you were in the ground? he asks.

No.

Eight weeks, he says, and she looks surprised, her eyes climbing the hill as though looking for something.

Oh, she says.

He met her on TV. She was already dead by then: in all the photographs beautiful, smiling, nineteen. She was buried a mile from his apartment and he went to her every night, all night. The facts of her death did not deter him: *brutal, raped, slashed.* His love would fix all that. All she had to do was find her way back to the world, to him. If he wished hard enough, loved strong enough, she would. Did.

When he kisses her he can taste her teeth right behind her lips. There is no water in her; she can't cry, she can't spit. Everything on her cracks and splits. When he touches her he can feel her bones trying to remember how to move, clicking where the cartilage is almost gone.

Do you like it when I do this? he asks.

I will, she says, I just have to get used to it.

Am I your first?

She frowns. Why does that matter?

It doesn't, I just want to know.

Well, you know what he did, she tells him.

I mean besides what he did.

Then you're the first, she says, and he squeezes her hand, so happy. He says it: I'm happy.

She touches the hem of her dress, remembering something about it. Picking it out, putting it on. Being happy, too. She couldn't reach the zipper herself and someone had to zip it for her and that must be the sound she hears all the time, the teeth coming together, then being torn apart.

The cut is still there, a dark smile on her throat, but on the third night he can see something bright glitter beneath the skin: freshness, red.

There's blood, he says.

What?

Growing, inside. Can't you feel it?

She swallows. The spot shifts, looks wet.

No, she says. She touches the white line of skin on her ring finger.

Not there, he says. Here. On your neck.

I can't feel anything there.

Just try.

No, she says again, and pushes his hand away, the

bone-light brush of her without power, without weight. He thinks of holding her wrist, squeezing it. It would snap. Even a man like him would be able to hurt her. The other man, the bad one, was so big he could do anything. Whatever he wanted.

She looks tired, or maybe it's just how deep her eyes have sunk in their sockets. It's hard for her to really look at him; she keeps seeing old things, things that aren't happening anymore, and the new things get lost beneath them. He tells her that her vision will get better; she knows it won't, because her eyes aren't really eyes anymore, but she keeps this to herself. They sit on the dark grass and he holds her hand, marvels at it, the split nails still flecked with polish, pink. There are lots of little things like this, things that delight him: the full white skirt of her dress, the ankle straps on her white shoes, the small gold hoops in her ears.

Did you know? That I was here? I came every night. I read you all the articles and the obituaries and stuff, remember?

She nods. She doesn't say what else she heard: the dropping of his semen in the dirt, its slow sinking, the thirsty earth bringing it closer. The box stopped it from touching her but she still knew it was there, more and more, his crying out a whisper bleeding down to the roots of the new grass.

She shivers and he puts his arm around her. She can't seem to be made warm but he tries; he holds her close, closer, and she makes a sound and it sounds to him like Yes.

He can't take her out during the day—when the sun appears she is simply not there, doesn't come back again until it is night—but in the dark she can pass as something still living. He is ecstatic when he sees her, less than a week later, changed; the bones don't press so painfully against the skin, her eyes have fattened in their sockets. He has brought a comb and he rakes the rest of the dirt from her hair until it gleams. The wind strokes the tall grass. When they take their first step beyond the cemetery he is delirious, full of plans.

We could go out, he says. Dancing, walking, wherever you wanted to go.

Oh no, she says, shaking her head. No, I don't think so.

Why not? It's almost closed up, he says, looking at her neck. And the dress fits now. You gained weight.

I don't weigh anything, she says matter-of-factly.

He smiles. If you say so.

She looks down the road outside the gate and stops, pulling on his hand.

What? he asks.

We shouldn't, she says.

Shouldn't what? You don't want to go out tonight?

I don't think I want to go out any night, she says.

Why not?

I should go back to where I came from.

But you came from the ground, he says, giving her a little smile as he gestures toward the cemetery.

Isn't that where I belong?

No, he says. Why would you even say that?

She looks over her shoulder, back to the hill, takes a few drifting steps to the gate; he takes her arm to stop her, his fingers meeting around the narrow bone.

You're not giving this a chance, he says.

A chance? she says, and there is that look again in her eyes, like she is seeing two things at once.

Look, he urges, I'll be with you the whole time. I won't let you out of my sight for one second.

She swallows and her throat makes a clicking sound. I don't want to get in a car, she says. It always happens in cars.

He doesn't ask, What happens? Fine, he says, shrugging. We can walk, it's just six blocks. A nice place. I promise, you'll like it. Okay?

She is quiet.

Okay? he says again.

He gets her a soda water with cranberry; he drinks bourbon straight. She looks at the glass.

I could have brought you a clean dress, he apologizes. I will next time.

She shakes her head. It's fine.

Take a sip, he suggests.

She puts the glass to her lips but the liquid somehow doesn't make it into her mouth. She can feel it dripping down the front of her. The cranberry juice leaves a long pink mark on her dress and she scratches at it with a napkin, over and over.

It's okay, he says, patting her knee. We'll try again some other time. Did you taste it at all? he asks.

I don't know, she says, and as she works at the stain her movements become angry, erratic. What is it supposed to taste like? she says.

What do you mean?

I can't drink it! she half-shouts, the scarf around her neck slipping; she pushes it back up.

Hey, he says, leaning close to calm her. Shh. There's nothing wrong.

Her fingers tremble. I still can't really see you, she says. I don't know what you look like.

Who cares, honey, you will, you'll see everything

just perfect in a little while, he says, draining his glass. I'll put a song on for you.

I don't want music, she says.

He tucks his lips, turns the glass in his hands. I didn't bring you here so you could mope.

What did you bring me here for?

To just . . . have a nice time. He shrugs. He can't say what he wants, it is so deep, so difficult inside him. It will take time, he reminds himself; he can wait, he has already been so patient.

Remember this? he says, slipping the ring out of his pocket, putting it on the bar. She stares at it: something flickers in the amethyst heart, the scratched gold band.

Where did you get that?

I found it, he says, grinning. He offers it like a piece of candy, in the palm of his hand. It might be a little big now, he says. But you'll grow into it.

I don't want to, she says.

Why not?

She keeps her hands clasped beneath the bar. He elbows her gently. Just take it, he says.

She remembers the box it came in, white velvet, stamped with the name of the jeweler in silver letters.

But why? she asks. Why should I take it?

Because it's yours, because it's pretty. Why does it matter? Why do you make a big deal out of every little thing?

I don't.

You're always complaining.

She is silent.

Hey, come on. You look beautiful. No one can tell what happened to you. Don't worry about it.

She turns back to him, her eyes fresh with tears; his chest clenches to see them. Water. Life.

It's not *that*, she says through gritted teeth. Her cheeks are fuller, rounder. He still can't believe how young she looks. Is. Was.

Can we try to have a good time? Please?

Yes, she says. I'm trying.

You don't know what life was like for me before I met you. I know you had it bad, at the end, but you came from a good family at least. Not me.

I'm sorry about that.

You could at least thank me.

She covers her face with her hands. He wonders what she is doing behind them—crying, or getting ready to scream. He looks around the room but no one is watching. He wipes his napkin against the damp bar.

You can go to the ladies' room and clean your face, you know, he says. You can get that crud out from under your nails. You can make an effort.

She gets up from the stool and walks across the empty

dance floor to the bathroom without moving her hands from her eyes.

When she doesn't come back after a quarter hour he goes to look for her, his knuckles sorry on the door. Hey, you okay? he calls. No answer. He knocks again. Please, I didn't mean it, just come out.

When he opens the door there is no one inside, just a circle of dirt in the wet sink.

She walks until the pavement gives way to tall trees and soft earth. This is a different place, not the cemetery, not the side of the other road, where he might go to look for her again. This way is steep; she claws her way upward, her shoes slipping over the leaves, until the lights from the town are dim and she can start to dig.

She remembers this: the feeling of the dirt beneath her nails, the taste of it tamped hard into her mouth as the soil sucked her dry. There are white things in this earth, pieces of young roots or teeth or bone; she still can't quite see. Instead she sees him, recalls the naked rage in his face when she threw the ring from the window, the ring he had given her, the ring she did not want. It is on her hand now, because of him, the other one, and she takes it off, throwing it once more into black grass.

Sitting in the shallow pit, scooping dirt over her legs like a blanket, she watches as the white dress darkens; there is no young man here, she tells herself, no ring, no knife. The dress is gone. If she is lucky, she, too, will disappear.

THE DADDY

Daddy comes over on Thursdays. My husband and son are out watching movies where people blow each other up. They have burgers afterward and buffalo wings and milkshakes and they talk about TV shows and girls and the latest bloody video game. At least that's what I imagine they do. No way do they imagine what I am doing, sitting here at the kitchen table doing my math homework as Daddy microwaves the mac and cheese he brought over. We have three hours together and in these three hours I am twelve years old and my daddy is the most wonderful man in the world.

———————

On craigslist I post the photo from my work website, the one with my hair scraped back in a ponytail, exposing my shiny forehead, my thin lips, my arms bursting from the sleeves of my blue blouse. *Daughter seeks Father* is all I write as a caption. In response I receive an avalanche of cell-phone numbers, chat invitations, and penis pics lifted from porn sites.

I delete all the emails except for Richard's: *Sweetheart, please call home.* I sit for a moment hunched in my cubicle, sweating, before lifting the receiver and dialing his number.

Daddy? I whisper, hand up to cover my mouth so no one walking by can see it moving.

He doesn't skip a beat. Sweetheart! he says.

Did you see the photo? I ask.

Of course, he says.

I'm not better in person, I warn.

You're perfect, he assures me.

I'm married, I tell him. I have a kid.

No problem, he insists.

I chew the inside of my cheek. There's not going to be any sex, I say.

Absolutely not! he agrees.

I wait for him to say something creepy or disgusting, but he doesn't. We make arrangements to meet at McDonald's for dinner on Thursday.

Don't kill me, I say, and he laughs.

Oh sweetheart, he says. What on earth?

I'm early. I don't know what Daddy looks like and every time the door swings open my head jerks like a ball on a string. I convince myself I'm going to be stood up and that it will be better anyway if I am. But at seven on the dot he enters and he looks straight at me and waves.

Our usual, sweetheart? he says, loud enough for other people to hear, and I nod. He brings a tray of chicken nugget combos to my table. He kisses my cheek. The food steams in our hands as we look at each other; he seems about twenty, twenty-two, with chinos frayed at the bottoms and red hair and glasses and biceps as skinny as my wrist. Maybe someday he will be good-looking.

Extra barbecue sauce, just the way you like, he says, gesturing to my nuggets. I smile and take a bite. He asks me about school and I ask him about work and he is as interested in how I'm doing in gym class as I am in the stocks he's trading at the office; we slip into our new roles as easily as knives into butter.

I almost forgot, he says. He reaches into the pocket of his jacket and pulls out a CD with a Christmas bow stuck on it. Just a little something, he adds, and hands it to me. I unstick the bow and turn the CD over in my hands: Britney Spears. I bounce, once, and my left butt cheek, which doesn't quite fit on the plastic chair, bangs on the edge of the seat.

Oh Daddy, I say, touched because I know he went into a store and asked what would be the right thing to get for his little girl, and he paid for it with his own money and put it in his pocket and found the gaudy bow to go with it and then brought it all the way here, to me, because he knew he would like me and already wanted to give me something, and this makes me want to give everything I have to him in return.

Apart from Thursday nights—and it's always Thursdays, always nights—we don't communicate, except by email. Sometimes he'll send me a note just to say, *Have a great day!!* or he'll tell me what plans he has for dinner: *Working late need a treat pizza sound good???* or he'll hint at imagined happenings in my little-girl life: *Don't forget dentist today xoxoxoxo!!* and *Good luck on the history quiz I know you'll do awesome!!!!* I write back in equally breathless terms to report the results of the history quiz or the number of cavities rotting my teeth or to squeal over the impending pizza feast. These exchanges give me a high so intense my chest muscles spasm and when my boss calls and says to bring her such-and-such a document I hit print and out comes an email from Daddy, not the work document, and I giggle into my hand and hit print again.

He always arrives exactly fifteen minutes after my husband and son leave. I sit on the couch with the television on while he fumbles with the keys and the empty banged-up briefcase he always brings. *Sweetheart!* he says when he enters, and I yelp *Daddy!* and if I was maybe ten or twenty or, okay, thirty pounds lighter, I might run toward him, but as it is I wait on the couch for him to come over and kiss my hair. I'll pour him a soda on the rocks and he'll pour me some milk and we touch glasses and smile. If my husband calls I stand by the back door with my head down and say Uh-huh, yes, fine, all right, see you soon, no, nothing for me, thanks, I'm enjoying the leftovers, have fun, love you.

Richard lives with his mother but I never meet her or hear anything about her. I only know she exists because I Google Richard's phone number and thanks to the white pages I know where he lives. She is seven years older than me and her name is Gayle. I imagine Richard when he is not Daddy, lurking unhappily beneath her thumb, still living in the room he grew up in. I wonder if he's done his homework and discovered that I am a loser, too. Or maybe it's obvious and he doesn't care. So when I'm with him I don't care either.

We never run out of things to talk about. There are dance recitals and music lessons and colds and heartbreaks to discuss and I am always the center of his attention. Sometimes he comes and crouches by the sink and pretends to fix a faulty pipe; I stand helpful at his side and listen to him slap and pull at the plastic tubes. Other times I refuse to do my homework or flaunt the fact that I've ignored my chores and he has to speak very sternly to me and point at the neglected essay assignment or the pile of dirty laundry in the middle of the floor until I melt with shame. He is patient and fair and my tantrums are mild, my rebellions quickly conquered. Sometimes, if I'm feeling low that week, I will cry for real, and he'll say There are lots of other boys who will want to go to the dance with you, or You can always try out next year for the team, or—and this is by far my favorite—The school photo came out beautiful. And I sniff and say Really? It did? And he literally dries my tears with his hands and says Yes, of course it did.

———

Some girls are being mean to me, I complain one Thursday. Daddy whips his head up from his food like a hunting dog smelling blood. Excuse me? he says. Who exactly is being mean to you?

Jennifer and Holly and Deborah, I say, using the names of women from work, women who aren't mean to me but might as well be since they are not and never will be my friends.

He shakes his head, wiping his fingers with his napkin before leaning back in his chair, his wrists on either side of his plate.

That is unacceptable, he says. When did this start?

I shrug. They've always had something against me.

Do I need to call the school? Do I need to have a conference with their parents?

Maybe, I say. It's just not fair that they're so stupid but everyone thinks they're so cute.

No one's cuter than you.

You're just saying that.

He puts his hand on mine. You are the most beautiful, wonderful, most talented girl I know.

You must not know a lot of girls, I joke.

I'm serious, Kathleen. Don't let anyone tell you otherwise, okay?

Okay, I say.

Promise, he insists.

I promise, I say, giggling.

He isn't laughing. Swear, he says, and I sober up, look into his eyes, and swear.

There are a few times when Daddy seems tired and we go out to eat and he sits there slushing his straw through his Diet Coke. Those Thursdays we're alone with our private miseries, just like every father and daughter in the world, and the feeling is tender and beautiful. What's wrong, Daddy, I'll ask, and he taps my hand with his fingers and musters a smile and says Nothing you need to worry about, sweetheart, and I'll suggest a long drive and sundaes to go. His car is old and strewn with trash and I sing along to the radio and Daddy sings too and when he drops me off he touches my cheek and says Sunshine, you always know just how to cheer me up. Then we both get teary from loving each other so much and I go into my house and wave from the window and watch him drive away.

I'm in the bathroom at work trying to masturbate. I have good enough sex at home but nevertheless there is a gaping hole in me somewhere that says *Do something.* If it's not sex and not food and not a night out with the girls then what is it that I need? What is the nature of this hole and with what do I seal it up? When Daddy comes home I am bursting with gratitude but when he leaves I am starving, I literally feel my mouth fill with saliva and I think with agony there are a maximum of hours to get through before the next Thursday evening. In the bathroom my hand sweats between my legs and I imagine Daddy gently pointing out to me everything I've got wrong and then coaching me on how to get it right. I wonder for a second if the no-sex clause was a mistake, but when I think about sex with Richard my hand flees from my crotch like it's been scalded. I shake it, wanting to yell at it, yell at myself *What the fuck-hell are you doing. You useless, you failure, you sad cow.* I yank my pants up over my hips and stuff my shirt in. Someone comes into the bathroom and I look through the gap of the stall door and see Deborah, my manager, wetting her fingers and then touching her bangs. She looks cool as a cucumber. I want to ask her How? and Why you? and then Why you and not me? But then I remind myself of Thursday night and I remember that getting off is something everyone does, one way or another, but Daddy is something that no one has, not even Deborah, and this is significant. I take a deep breath and exit the stall. The naughty hand is red and moist but I don't worry about whether Deborah thinks I am weird or sad. She keeps staring at her own reflection and I snap two towels from the dispenser and dry myself and hear Daddy saying to me Kathleen, don't cry. So I don't.

———

At dinner I bend over the table and wince. Richard half-rises, touching my arm.

Are you okay, sweetheart?

My stomach hurts, I say.

Is it something you ate?

I don't know.

Why don't you try using the toilet, he suggests. I hobble to the bathroom. I'm in there a long time, and when he knocks I don't answer. He eases the door open. I am staring into the toilet, where blood unspools in the water. He takes a deep breath.

You started, he says. Hey, that's great, right? Does it hurt a lot?

I nod. He takes my arm, opens the drawer I've stocked with Tampax in neon wrappers designed to appeal to teens. Solemnly, sweetly, he removes a tampon and hands it to me.

Do you know where to put this?

I bite my lip.

See here, on the box? He tilts it for me to see the drawing of a girl inserting a tampon into her penciled vagina. You take this and unwrap it. This part is the applicator and you use it to push this part—the cotton thing, see?—inside. Okay?

He caresses my arm, peering up into my face before leaving me in the bathroom alone. I hold the tampon in my fist and close my eyes as I squat over the toilet and push the tampon in. I know he's standing outside the door, listening, waiting. I want to cry out, but I don't. The tampon swells slowly inside me. I open the bathroom door. Daddy uncrosses his arms, pushes his glasses up on his nose.

Okay? he says.

Okay, I say, with a small smile, and he hugs me, his chin against my hair, and we stay that way for the next minute or so, and then he gives me a last little squeeze and we return to the kitchen for ice cream straight out of the container before he sends me to bed.

I know, thanks to LinkedIn, that Richard is a math major at the community college and I want to ask him if he knows anything about statistics and so could he tell me what the numbers are about people like us: how many in a town our size? In our state? In our country? What does *like us* even mean? Come Thursdays I am ready to self-medicate up to my eyeballs in Daddy's laughter, his wrinkled khakis, his drives to the Dairy Queen for vanilla cones, and he never tells me to want anything else or anything less. We are special. We are us. We clasp hands and laugh and Daddy pays the bill, and when we get to the car again he has me do a little twirl under his arm, and even in old pants and clogs with the heels rubbed raw I shine.

————

In the time I know Richard I gain weight and I am not promoted at work and I appreciate my husband less and less for the solid unremarkable man that he is, and maybe you could say that this means the whole Daddy thing is a failure but I would never say that. I don't know what having a daughter does for Richard exactly, though in the back of my mind are vague hopes for him: that he graduates, that he gets a good job, that he finds his own place. But the thought of him having children slices me in half. If my mind happens to dig up this thought I spend the rest of the day trying to pull my cut-apart halves together again. He's young, he could be impotent, it's likely he'll never even get a girlfriend, but still I'm sore where the thought of other daughters has severed me so completely and I have to add that ache to all the other aches, and by the end of my adding I am exhausted and have to lie down, and then my husband complains that I am lazy, that the dishes are dirty, that his job is harder than mine so what am I complaining about? And I say I am not complaining, I am simply lying down, and he says Same thing.

It's supposed to be a "date": dinner at a real Italian place and tickets to a movie starring a popular teenage singer. Maybe unconsciously I want to spice things up. Maybe nothing is ever good enough for me and that's why I answer the door in a strapless dress that hits just above the knee. My hair is teased high around my face and my feet are crammed into red patent heels and my legs are blistered raw from a hasty shave job. Daddy stares and I stare back and I can see that he is surprised but up to the challenge.

What do you think you're doing, young lady? he demands, stepping quickly into the house and shutting the door.

Nothing, I mumble.

Nothing? he scoffs. Look at yourself.

You don't like it? I ask, knuckling the sweat off my upper lip.

You need to change, he says. Now.

No, I say.

Yes, he insists.

I don't want to.

I didn't ask you if you wanted to, I *told* you to.

I stamp my foot. But it's pretty and I want to wear it.

I said *change*, he repeats, and grips my arm, not nicely; instantly a wildness burns into being in both of us, or maybe it was always there, ready for this moment. I rip my arm from his hand and wave it in the air.

I look nice! I shout.

You look ridiculous! he yells back, pushing his glasses up his nose, pointing to the bedroom door.

Go cover up!

No!

Yes! Right now!

Why?

Because it's—inappropriate!

But everyone dresses like this! It's not fair!

He puts his hands on his hips and his jaw is tight and his pale lips are flecked with spit.

You are not everyone, you are my daughter, and you will do as I say!

You can't tell me what to do!

Kathleen Anne Marie Masterson! he shouts, so loud I take a step back. Get in your room and change your clothes this instant or I—

You'll what? I dare him.

I'll ground you for a month! he hisses.

Go ahead! I don't care!

He folds his arms. We are not leaving this house until you take off that dress and wash that junk off your face, he says, his voice cracking. When his eyes cut to anywhere below my chin he winces; I want to hold on to the agony of these clothes, these cheap shoes, my pitiful flesh, and he wants to spare me. He reaches out his hand and tries to wipe away my lipstick; I toss my head like a rabid horse.

Stop it! Leave me alone!

His thumb keeps driving toward my mouth and finally I bite him, quick; the taste of Daddy is like erasers or sweating paper. He yelps and I take a step back, licking my lips.

Why do you want to look like a whore? Are you a whore? he yells. The words are like lightning between us, splitting us open: beneath the staleness of the parts we are playing we are truly shocked, outraged, crazed. He shakes his hand to rid himself of the sting of my bite and as he does I remember my own hand, in the bathroom, rubbing, wet. I realize that he has an erection. I don't look away fast enough and he sees me seeing it, and we both just stop.

Fine, I whisper, and hurry to my room to change, ripping the dress down and off before balling it beneath the bed. I scrub at my eyes and mouth with a towel, then mash the moussed-up rings into a ponytail and stick my feet into my sneakers. I'm gulping air; I have to lean against the dresser for a while before I'm able to go back to Daddy, who is sitting on the couch staring at the blank television, or maybe at the photo of my son on top of it; I can see myself in the black glass of the high school portrait, a ghost figure next to my son's smiling head.

I'm ready, I say. He turns and I see his eyes cramped behind his glasses, gentle and miserable. Something has been chipped from both of us, accidentally, necessarily, but I don't know how big the chip is yet, or if, by now, we can afford to lose it.

Is this better? I ask.

Yes, thank you, Katie, he says, and I follow him out the door with my head bowed, trembling like a bride.

I call Daddy at two in the morning, standing in my driveway with no jacket or shoes, shivering.

Sweetheart? he answers.

I blubber wordlessly into the phone.

Honey, have you been drinking alcohol?

No, I say. Yes.

You shouldn't do that, he says.

I know, I say, on a shaky exhale, wiping my nose with the back of my hand. I think of him in his apartment, his mother in the other room. When he answered the phone he sounded wide awake; maybe he was watching TV or playing video games, not thinking about being Daddy, just being a nobody.

What is it? he says.

I squeeze my eyes shut and whisper without thinking.

I wish you were my real dad.

I am, he says, not in his Daddy voice but in a Richard voice I have never heard before, thin and uncertain. I hang up. He calls back and I don't answer and there is just one word in the message he leaves in the new small voice I don't recognize and don't want: Sorry.

The next morning I am hungover but hopeful. So we had a little misstep. So I blew things out of proportion. So I made a fool of myself—it's nothing Daddy can't fix. I clean the house and iron my jeans, read a teen gossip magazine. I am looking somewhat prettier than usual and I wonder if he will bring a present, as he sometimes does. I hope for a necklace or a bottle of scented lotion.

At six Daddy calls to say he can't make it because of a last-minute meeting with a big client. He's trying to sound cheerful, but we both hear Richard panicking. Maybe you can call in a pizza? he suggests weakly. I say yeah, maybe. I don't ask if he'll be home in time to tuck me in; we don't say we love each other, we don't say anything else, except he says Take care. And then I know for sure that it's over.

Hours later I'm waiting on the couch when my husband comes home with my son, laughing, both of them high on football and Red Bull. I tell them to take off their shoes. My husband flops on the couch. I hand over the remote and he flips to the sports.

I hear my son rummaging in the fridge, whooping when he finds the pizza I ordered but didn't eat still in its box. He stands in the doorway, chewing with his mouth open, Daddy's slice devoured in three bites.

We stay here like this, my husband's hand on my knee, my son wiping his fingers on his shirt, and I think, This is it, this is Thursday from now on, and as I start to cry I hear Daddy's voice, tired and unimpressed, saying, *Grow up, Kathleen, grow up grow up grow up.*

RAPTURE

The man is brushing his teeth when the doorbell rings. Pausing, he listens: it is not even light out yet. The doorbell rings again, and the man sets his toothbrush down on the edge of the sink, wiping his mouth on the towel.

The man opens the door. Standing on the mat is a boy, ten or eleven years old, in jeans and a brown sweater, a newspaper at his feet.

Oh, the man says. Are you the new paperboy?

No, the boy says.

Oh, the man says again.

I have something that's yours.

You do?

The boy nods.

Well—what is it?

I have to go inside your house to show you, the boy says.

My house? the man echoes.

Can I?

The man turns to look over his shoulder, into the empty hall, then turns back to the boy.

Okay—

The boy walks in, flattening past the man.

Close the door, the boy says.

The man closes it.

Do I know you? the man asks. I mean, have we met before?

No, the boy says.

Don't you have school?

The boy shakes his head. Not today.

Who knows you're here?

The boy looks at him, his eyes glittering in a face made of milk and bone.

No one, the boy says.

The house is ordinary; it used to belong to the man's parents, and almost everything in it is theirs. The man's computer and desk stand where the piano used to be, and the shape the piano left on the wallpaper doesn't match the shapes of the new furniture.

The boy slips a canvas bag from his shoulder to the floor, sweeping the room with his eyes.

You need to give me something? the man asks.

There was a package for you, the boy says.

What package?

This, the boy says, pulling a plain black DVD case from his bag.

That's mine?

The boy nods.

The blood in the man's face burns. Then why would you take it? If it wasn't yours?

Just because.

Because why?

Is it something secret? the boy asks.

The man's surprise turns cold.

It's not for children, he says.

I want to see it, the boy insists.

No, the man says.

I have the envelope, the boy threatens. With your name on it.

The man opens his mouth. The boy moves deeper into the house.

The man sits down at the desk and taps the computer awake. The boy stands at his elbow; the man swallows. He loads the disc into the player.

On-screen a boy begins hitting a man bound to a

chair. Both are naked, except for a pair of boots laced to the boy's knees. The boy slaps the man, over and over. The man's eyes are half-closed and he makes no sound. The boy shoves the man's head back and spits into his mouth.

Before anything else can happen, the real man punches a key on the keyboard; the figures on the screen freeze.

Why did you stop it? the boy asks.

The man shakes his head.

I shouldn't show it to you, the man says.

Why not?

It's bad.

Why?

Because.

Because why?

Because it's not normal.

But it's just pretend.

The man pauses. Yes, he says. But even pretend things should be the right things.

Why?

The man moves to shut down the computer but the boy pushes the man's hand away. The man leans back in the chair.

Because, the man says again.

Why do you like it?

I don't like it.

You don't?

Can I turn it off now?

The boy's eyes flicker over the still image. Okay, he says, and the man leans forward, fast. The screen crackles.

Is that all? the man asks.

All what?

All you wanted?

The boy rolls his lip between his teeth. The man moves his chair a little, back and forth.

No, the boy says finally.

They stay, still, the man in his chair and the boy standing beside him, watching, waiting.

I want to look around, the boy says.

The man makes a soft sound, not quite a laugh.

Why? What are you looking for?

The boy shrugs.

The man's bedroom is jammed with clothes, tangled blankets, paper. The blinds are shut and the curtains drawn.

It's messy, the boy says.

No one comes in here usually, the man explains from the doorway.

The boy slides open the closet door, touching the

man's clothes, moving a shoe with his foot. He inspects a broken lamp, a bookcase of paperbacks. He opens the dresser, exposing twin stacks of white shorts.

The boy looks into the nightstand drawer. The man holds his breath. There are pictures inside the drawer, which the boy shuffles without comment.

Will you tell? the man asks.

The boy shakes his head, easing the drawer shut. On the nightstand is an alarm clock, a water glass, and several bottles of pills; the boy touches his finger to each one.

What do you take this for? he asks.

Stomachaches, the man answers.

And this one?

Blood pressure.

And this?

The man hesitates. To feel better, he says.

Feel better how?

It's for depression, the man says.

The boy moves the bottle to the edge of the table with his finger on the cap.

Do you ever get sad? the man asks.

Everyone gets sad, the boy says.

That's true, the man says.

From a vent in the wall comes a hollow boom; the boy whips his head around.

What was that?

The heat coming on. Did it scare you?

No, the boy says, and turns back to the nightstand.

You don't get scared, the man says, turning his shoulder into the doorjamb.

That's right.

You're like—an animal.

The boy cocks his head. What kind?

I don't know. One that doesn't have a name yet.

The boy is pleased. He shows his teeth.

I'm going to have some juice, the man says. Would you like some?

The boy follows the man into the kitchen and sits at the table, tapping his knuckles on the Formica.

Do you like orange? Or grape? the man asks.

Orange, the boy says. He watches as the man moves around opening cabinets, pulling out glasses, pouring juice.

What is your job? the boy asks.

I do people's taxes, he says. Do you know what that is?

Yes, the boy says.

The man watches from the corner of his eye as the boy's arm darts forward to take an envelope from a stack of unopened mail.

Here you go, the man says. The boy tilts the glass to look inside before taking a sip.

What would you have done today if I hadn't come?

Oh, the man says. Probably done my grocery shopping.

We can do that, the boy says.

You want to go to the store with me?

Yes. I want to choose what we have for dinner.

The man opens his mouth, closes, it, opens it again.

You're staying for dinner?

The boy nods, sliding his finger into the envelope and pulling out the paper inside.

You owe thirty-nine dollars to the gas company, the boy says, smoothing the paper with both hands.

The man rubs juice off his lip, twisting his head to look at the bill.

Hm. That's not too bad.

The boy thinks of a menu, makes a list. They discuss how much things will cost, how much money the man has, what coupons they can use from those pinned to the fridge.

You figured this out like a grown-up, the man says.

I'm not stupid.

Of course not.

I know what you are, the boy says, and the man sits back.

What I am?

The boy nods, his lips pulled in. Everyone knows it.

Oh, the man says. Everyone?

Well, a lot of people.

What do they know?

The boy looks at him, shrugs.

I've never done anything wrong, the man says.

The boy says nothing.

Do people know about you? the man asks.

What about me?

That you steal, the man says gently. That you break into people's houses.

The boy lifts his chin. I gave the movie back. And I asked to come in.

The man nods. Yes. You're right. You did.

Are you mad?

No, the man says. I'm not mad.

The man pushes the cart and the boy consults his list. They get eggs and low-fat milk and chicken breasts and frozen peas, frozen corn, frozen fish. When they get to the desserts the man stops, drumming the cart handle with his palms.

What about ice cream? he asks.

The boy peers into the freezer bin and sighs. Well, maybe we could get one kind. The small one.

Chocolate?

The boy shakes his head. Vanilla is better.

Okay, the man says, and the boy puts the carton in between the corn and the fish.

They finish their shopping, weaving through each aisle with slow steps. The man notices that some people are looking, people he recognizes and people who maybe recognize the boy. The boy seems to notice nothing.

They unload the cart together and the boy pulls out the man's wallet and pays, laying each bill out one by one.

The cashier smiles. You're in charge today, huh? she says.

I'd like plastic, please, the boy says. He folds the wallet and puts it into his own pocket.

Do you ever go out on dates? the boy asks as they put the grocery bags into the trunk of the man's car. The man opens the door for the boy, closes it, walks around to the driver's side, gets in.

Not really, the man says. Do you?

The boy raises his eyebrows.

No, he says. Of course not.

Oh well, someday, the man says.

Even if you don't like girls you can go out on dates with boys, the boy says.

The man's knee jerks, hitting the underside of the dashboard.

I don't think so, he says.

Why not?

Because, he says.

The man turns into the street. He stops at a light, looking into the crosswalk.

You know, he says suddenly, into the shell of the boy's silence, his hands gripping the top of the steering wheel. Right now everything is fine. Everything is how I would want it if I could choose and in life those are the moments that matter and I hope your whole life is like that.

But he doesn't say the last part. He just says, You know, and stops. The light turns green. Instead he says It's easy to talk to you about things.

The boy nods. The boy knows everything. He is not human. He is a child.

The man bakes chicken according to the boy's directions: white sauce and peas and noodles poured into a casserole dish. While it's cooking they watch the news, side by side on the couch, the man's arm over the back of the boy's cushion. There are stories about fires, robberies, unsolved murders; the man is surprised not to see his own face on the screen, or the face of the boy.

Are you allowed to watch this? the man asks.

Sure, the boy says.

It's very violent.

It's just the news, the boy says. Anyone can watch it.

The man sets the table. The room smells like meat and cream. They both drink milk.

It's good, the boy says.

I think so, too, the man says. Do you eat this at home?

The boy shrugs.

You haven't said anything about yourself, the man says. What grade you're in or what sports you play or anything like that.

The boy continues to eat, scraping his plate.

Do you have a favorite TV show?

The boy looks at the man. No, he says.

For dessert the boy scoops out ice cream from the small container. The boy looks back and forth between the bowls to make sure each serving is the same.

What are you thinking about? the man asks.

Your video, the boy says, his spoon slicing through the pale planet of ice cream.

Did you like it? the man asks.

Reaching over the table, his hips lifted from the

chair, the boy slaps the man, and then he puts his hands on the man's face and keeps them there. The man is perfectly still. Helpless. The boy touches the man's cheeks, his mouth, his nose, his brow. Through the bars of the boy's fingers the man can see the boy's gray eyes, his unsmiling lips.

The telephone rings. The boy doesn't move his hands away.

Are you going to answer it? the boy asks.

No, the man says. They listen to the phone tap the silence to pieces, six, seven times. Then the ringing stops.

The man washes the dishes and the boy dries. They work without speaking, the man plunging cups and knives into the gray water, the boy twisting a towel inside the bowls. The last plate slips from the boy's hand and onto the floor, splitting into a constellation of white glass.

I'm sorry, the boy says.

It's all right, the man replies.

He takes the boy by the shoulders and steers him around the broken plate and into the living room. The faces on the television screen move quietly; the light from the lamps puddles on the red carpets.

The boy offers his hand, and the man takes it; it is

like a fish or a bird, restless, small. He cannot hold it for long.

Goodbye, the boy says, pulling his bag over his shoulder. The man stands in the open mouth of his house, watching the boy step off the porch. He wants to ask if the boy got what he came for. What did you come for? But the boy is already on the lawn, his sneakers leaving tracks in the damp grass, and then he is gone.

STONES

At Beanie's she is filling in for the old man who usually handles the takeout orders. Kevin gives her his name; she puts his food on the counter but doesn't push it toward him or tell him what he owes. She just stands there, staring. He puts some money down and she shoves it, unsorted, into the cash drawer.

I've seen you in here before, she says in a low voice, leaning forward, her blouse bunching against the counter. She is smiling, but he doesn't see the smile; he is looking at her blouse touching the filthy countertop. His eye twitches.

You want my number? she asks, and before he can answer she is writing it across the lid of the takeout box with a red pen plucked from the cup next to the register. The Styrofoam squeaks beneath her fingers, and she slaps the cap of the pen into place, ties the bag shut, and winks.

Enjoy your lunch, she says. As she walks into the dining room he sees the deformed foot, her right one, twisting inward at the ankle, dragging behind the left.

He is eating the sandwich in his car, staring at the numbers on the box, when his phone rings. When he answers all she does at first is breathe.

How did you get my number? he whispers.

Why didn't you call? she replies.

I was going to, he says, checking his watch: twenty minutes since he left the restaurant.

Well it's my break now, she says, and he can tell she has her hand cupped around the mouthpiece of the phone; her breath pops against his ear. Are you listening? she asks.

Yes, he says.

She tells him: Drive to one of the many shitty parts of town and park on the street. A single rock on the concrete driveway means that she is home and waiting. No rock, and it means one of the boys is there, or she is gone on an errand or is working the tables at Beanie's.

If he sees the stone, he is to go in through the side door, which will be open, and find her.

Outside of her waitressing uniform she is like a toothpick from which something has melted, her pale scanty flesh sponge-like, unmuscled. Her breasts sink, braless, beneath the thin cotton of a T-shirt. She has no pants on, just a pair of beige bikini underwear, revealing a leg bisected at the shin by a deep, thick scar flanked by a half dozen smaller ones, silver and slightly shiny. But the leg is nothing compared to the foot itself: the mashed-looking anklebone, the swollen instep twice the size of the normal foot, hideously warped.

Her uncombed hair hangs loose to her shoulders; she's leaning against the oven, makeup in the wrong colors scratched over her skinny face. He cannot stop looking at her.

You came, she says.

He nods.

Did you bring it?

He pulls the stone from his shirt pocket. It's squarish, a quarter the size of his palm, gritty, white—quartz, maybe. She lifts herself up on the counter next to the stovetop and pulls her panties aside.

Go ahead, she says.

He hesitates. Maybe I should wash it off first?

Don't bother.

It's got some dirt on it—

No, it's fine, just do it, she urges, grabbing his wrist and yanking it down to her crotch. He holds his breath.

Don't look down, just feel.

He steps in close and rubs the rock against her, the hair between her legs prickling his fingertips. Her hips move and his hand moves with them; as she slickens he relaxes, letting the stone go where it wants. When she told him about it on the phone, about this thing that she wanted him to do, it had sounded awkward, impossible, but in reality it happens without effort; the stone is between his fingers and then it's inside her.

You're so good, she sighs into his ear, her arm hanging down his back. He exhales, his mouth open against the tough button of her nipple.

Yeah? he says.

Yeah, she answers, and he feels how loose her legs go when he does it, the sound of her shirt crawling up and down the cabinet as she rides the side of his hand. Okay, he keeps saying. Okay okay.

Suddenly she grips his shoulder, every part of her going tight. He shivers. It takes her a while to focus on his face; when she does she smiles, pats his arm.

Is that—it? he asks, panting.

That's it, she replies, sliding off the counter, easing

the good foot down first. Want a drink? He looks at her foot, then at his hand.

Um, he says.

She yanks open the refrigerator door, sighing as she surveys its contents. We got wine, beer, or Diet Coke.

He's still looking at his hand, not knowing what the protocol is for cleaning a woman off one's fingers: wash, wipe, or air dry? She pours them both sodas and gives him one; his fingers slide on the plastic cup.

Cheers, she says.

They are at the kitchen table when the boys come in, slinging their backpacks into the hallway before turning into the kitchen. When they see Kevin sipping a Diet Coke across from their mother, they freeze.

Whoa! Quasimodo!

Nicole grimaces. Cut it out, she mumbles around her cigarette.

They approach Kevin in delighted disbelief, close enough for him to smell their sour breath.

Shit, what happened to your back?

Nothing, Kevin says.

It's like a giant fucking tit under there, seriously, they say. Fucking double D!

Hey, I said cut it out, she says.

What? they say, innocent. Give us a ciggie, Nic.

Mom, she corrects them.

Nic, they insist, grinning. She tosses the cigarette pack in their direction.

There's ham in the fridge, she says. And chips.

The boys nudge each other. *Tit*, they whisper, then guffaw hysterically as they pile food into their arms. They are much bigger than their mother, black-haired, athletic, baggy pants lashed to their hips by thick belts, the hoods of their sweatshirts up despite the heat.

Those're the twins, she says, with a smile somewhere between pride and apology.

Oh, he says.

When the boys are done raiding the cabinets they turn toward him, smirking, hands full.

Nice to meet you, Tit.

Nicole shakes her head. Kevin doesn't say anything, just looks at the wall. Somewhere inside their mother is a rock, and he thinks about all the other things that must have been inside her: cocks, tampons, smaller versions of the boys. He winces at the wallpaper. He hears her thumb on the cigarette, tipping ash into an empty Doritos bag.

They're good boys, really, she says.

They go from one rock to a half dozen, then a dozen. He doesn't know what it feels like for her, how it can feel good; there is something, maybe a lot of things, about female anatomy he doesn't understand, though he knows without asking how fast to go, how many stones to use, when to stop.

But when he is finished with the stones, when she has eased herself from the counter or the couch or the bed and he is waiting to be told what to do next, he wonders what they are: friends, or girlfriend and boyfriend, or something else? They don't go out to restaurants or bars or parties; he doesn't sleep over. She never comes to his apartment or gets into his car. He sees her at Beanie's, and he sees her here. That's it.

What they do—or, rather, what she does—is talk. She talks and talks, as soon as it is over, poking at her hair and smoking at the Formica table, drinking boxed wine with ice or diet soda or both, digging Corn Nuts from a bowl. Listening to her is the price of the pleasure he gets from the stones, and he submits to it, doglike, hunched on the hard seat.

In high school I fucked everyone, you know? she says, her voice mild, casual, smoke oozing from her mouth.

He blinks.

Not on purpose, she continues. It just kept happening. I mean, I was in a certain group and within that group everyone seemed to be doing that and I did it the most, I guess. She draws her good foot up on the table so she can pick a scab on her knee. The boys, they're sixteen.

Next to them I'm a fucking fossil. You'd never guess I'm in my thirties. *Early* thirties. I see some girls I went to school with and I used to be so much prettier than them and now they don't even look me in the face. You know, the ones who never had kids.

She stops for a moment and stares at her cup, then drains it.

Nicole, he says.

Hm, she says, brushing ash into her hand.

What happened to your foot? he asks.

She pauses, forehead tucking into a deep frown. What?

Your foot.

An accident, she says, enunciating carefully, tipping the ash in her hand onto the floor. She lights another cigarette.

Were you drunk?

She inhales, holds the smoke in her lungs. They stare at each other, and then there is a sound outside, of the boys shuffling up the porch, and she sits up immediately, smashing her cigarette out against the table.

Hi? she calls, like a question, craning to look into the hall. The boys go straight to their room. Nicole stays tilted in the chair for a moment, the vein in her neck pulsing. For the first time he notices a scar on her forehead, a fine porcelain line beneath her bangs.

Well, she says, settling the chair back on all fours. She draws another cigarette from the pack, lights it.

He wonders if anyone else ever notices it, placed so precisely, every time, in the center of the gray concrete. He parks at the curb, picks up the stone, puts his hand on the side door, pushes it open. The house smells like Nicole and the boys: fruity perfume and cigarettes, sour clothes, the stench of fast food and fried meat from Beanie's. But beneath all this he smells something else, the smell that comes from touching her, a smell that doesn't belong only to Nicole anymore but to him now, too.

He hears water running in the bathroom; he knocks.

Kevin? she calls.

Yeah, he says into the door. He imagines her in the shower, behind the plastic curtain beaded with black mold, scrubbing her scars. He has never seen her naked, never touched her anywhere except that one place.

Just get yourself a drink or whatever, she tells him. I'll be right out.

He wanders into the kitchen, fills a cup with water from the sink, sits. Darkness presses up against the windows, nibbles the edges of the weak kitchen light. A lingerie catalogue sits on the table beneath a plate of dried eggs and he looks at the cover model's legs. A moment later he hears them, her sons, coming into the house, and he freezes.

In the kitchen they grab cans of beer—not Nicole's beer, she sticks to wine, but their beer, beer they have convinced their mother to buy or that she has supplied without being asked; one of her little gifts to them, along with the cigarettes, the convenience foods, the absence of a curfew. They take a pizza from a box in the fridge, twist the dial on the oven. As they suck the foam from the top of the cans, their eyes roam through the room and finally land on him.

Shit, man, Titty's here.

Again? Dude, do you ever go home?

Nah, he's fucking Nic, like nonstop.

Ugh.

Fucking freak show, right? Gimp Nic and the Tit!

One of them imitates her shuffling step, leg turned in, arms flapping, eyes rolled up, while the other sticks his neck out and humps his brother's backside. They cry out in shattering falsettos; they grunt and slap and moan, they take turns playing Nicole, playing Kevin. It seems to go on and on, louder and louder, the big boys in their black clothes splashing through the room. Kevin shrinks against the wall. They crash into the kitchen chairs, knock their hips on the chrome edge of the table.

Stop, he says, stop it!

Their heads whip toward each other. It speaks! they crow.

You're disgusting, he whispers.

They laugh like they've been punched in the stomach.

What'd you say, Titty?

She's your mother.

So?

Where is your father? Kevin asks, glancing at them by accident. The boys stop laughing.

Our dad could kick your *ass*, they say.

But where is he? he repeats. The boys grunt, shout, shuffle, but they don't actually say anything. He stares at the brown door of the oven, where the pizza is dripping its cheese onto the red coils below the rack.

I think that's done, he says.

Asshole, they mutter, turning to pull the pizza from the oven with their bare hands, cursing as they attempt to shift the pizza to a plate before it buckles in half. As they slice the pie into pieces their mother walks in, bare-legged, scrubbing at her wet head with a towel.

Hey guys, she says. What're you making?

What's it look like, Nic.

She pinches Duncan's shoulder; the boy shrugs away.

I thought we could watch a movie later, she says.

They shake their heads, turning, plates of pizza pressed to their chests. We're going out.

But you just got back.

Things to do, Nic, they say, with big fake smiles. As they file past they look at Kevin, and their smiles harden.

Later, Titty.

The boys leave. Nicole finishes her hair, then goes to the oven, snapping the bake knob to Off.

Every time, she murmurs, and he can smell the cheese burning, can hear the boys laughing in the hall. She dips her head to wrap it into the towel, vertebrae spiking beneath the skin on her steam-flushed neck.

They're just kids, he says.

She turns, eyes wide. God, Kevin, I *know*.

She drags her foot to the fridge, gets a bottle of diet cola, pours it over ice into a plastic cup, then adds wine. Sitting opposite him she sips, running her little finger in circles over the tabletop. There is nothing for him to do here except watch her. The front door slams. She lights a cigarette.

What were you guys talking about?

He shrugs.

Did they give you shit or what?

He shrugs again.

Don't just sit there, say something!

What do you want me to say? he says, and she slaps him. Before he can even feel the sting her hand leaves on his cheek she is on her feet.

I'm sorry, fuck, Kevin, I'm sorry, I don't know why I'm like this, I really don't! she yelps, stubbing her cigarette out, her hand shaking as she begins clearing away the bags and empty cans that litter the tabletop. This place is a pit, she says, pulling the bin from beneath the sink. Can I make you a sandwich? Or we could order something. Chinese or whatever. I haven't eaten. I was waiting for the boys—

She's speaking to the garbage, trying to cram all the junk in. Duncan! Kenneth! she yells over her shoulder. Take this trash out now! I told you before!

They've gone out, Kevin reminds her.

She looks at him, mouth open, then turns back to the trash.

I'll take it, he says.

No, you—you don't have do anything, they should do it, I've told them to put this junk outside, I keep— she shoves again at the trash—telling them—

He gets up, lifts the can, takes it outside, dumps it into the bin. Bottles and cans crash atop more bottles and cans and the sound bounces away through the cul-de-sac, then rams back against him as he stands at the curb, his hands at the back of his hips, staring into the dark street; even though the streetlamp is out he can see all the little stones on the road. Rocks everywhere. He rolls one beneath the toe of his boot. He could get in his car and go home. He could turn off his phone, he could eat lunch somewhere else, he could stop coming to the driveway, to this house: that's what her men do, he guesses, they peel themselves away from her, they can't help it.

He stoops, picks up a rock. Puts it in his pocket.

In the morning he is still at her house, propped in a kitchen chair beside her bed, his head against the wall, mouth oozing saliva. She is sleeping, arm tossed high on the pillows. There is so much light coming in between the blinds on the windows he guesses it must be almost noon. He stands up carefully, his back sore, his stomach aching; they never did get any food last night, he'd just watched her drink and drink in the kitchen, and then he helped her to her room and she'd asked him to stay until she fell asleep. At the door he listens for the boys; their voices are barely audible, coming from somewhere outside. He goes to the hall bathroom; lifting the toilet seat he is met with a familiar film of piss on the porcelain. Afterward he looks for a toothbrush in the cabinet, but all he finds is an empty box of Band-Aids and several bottles of prescription pills. He reads the labels: her name, high dosages, pain. He closes the cabinet door, rinses his mouth with water from the tap.

When he returns to her room she is awake, sitting up

and smiling, girlish, her cheek scarred by the crumpled sheet.

Hi, she says. Sorry. Were you in the chair all night?

He shrugs, drifting in the doorway. She wipes her fingers beneath her eyes, collecting bits of mascara. The bad foot seems especially naked against the bedspread and he imagines putting his hand over it, just to feel it, to be nice to it.

Do you want to lie down for a minute?

He clears his throat. I thought I might go, actually.

Just for a minute, she says, slapping a pillow into shape. It won't kill you.

He goes to the bed. Leaning to rummage in the nightstand drawer she withdraws a handful of stones and once he has them in his hand he feels better; this is their territory. She lies back and pushes her underwear down and he leans in, the rocks in his fist, his knuckles brushing against her thighs, stirring the flesh between her legs. He bows his head. He does it as slow as he can, pushing the rocks up and up, one after another, a slow liquid press; there are eight, nine stones, and he uses them all. She closes her eyes. He rests his chin against her raised knee, her wetness drooling over his fingers. When the last one is in, his hand feels light, too light; she ends up with everything, he thinks, but that is the way it is, this is her one consolation.

Swallowing, she opens her eyes, reaching for him.

Come on, she breathes, her hair brushing his face, her sour breath hot on the crown of his head. Don't you want it?

She unzips him, draws him through the slit in his boxers. He sees that he is half-hard, but his penis is like a plant stapled to his crotch; he hardly recognizes it.

Keep touching me, she insists, wedging herself beneath him. He fumbles between her legs, all grace between them gone. Here, she's saying, Here, here, but he doesn't know what *here* means; his erection wanders, knocking against her bony pelvis, the crepey skin of her stomach. Her hand is down there as well, fishing out the pieces of quartz; they make an obscene sound as they land on the disintegrating carpet. He remembers the boys in the kitchen, chanting *Gimp Nic and the Tit*; he squeezes his eyes shut and groans.

It's okay, she says, pulling his hip to hers. There's room. See?

She thrusts upward; the tip of his penis sinks inside her and he feels immediately how wrong it is. There is nowhere for him to go.

What are you doing? she demands as, withdrawing, he watches himself wilt against her thigh.

I'm sorry, he says.

She drops her head back to the pillow. Shit, she breathes. He's frozen over her, his arms aching, his legs, bound at the knees by his jeans, like a tail between her thighs.

Lie down, she says, and pushes on his back, right on the hump, until he collapses. In his mind he is cutting off every part of himself that is touching her. She plucks the sheet up to their waists, her bad foot jutting sideways beneath the cover. The light stripes the bed, bends over their bodies. His despair floats somewhere above his head; he could reach up and touch it.

Look, she says, gazing through the window at her boys swinging baseball bats against the trunk of the leafless oak tree. The sound is ceaseless, cruel: *whack-shatter, whack-shatter*, pieces of bark shooting all the way to the window.

They're gorgeous, she whispers.

Yes, he says. She turns her back to him. The boys laugh. Bark bullets the glass.

THE CHEAT

We met near the Dumpster. I was on hall duty, which meant emptying all the trash from the dorms and common rooms into black sacks and dragging them out to the bins behind the kitchen. I kept hearing this crunching sound and I thought one of the other kids had nabbed a bag of Fritos, but when I looked around the Dumpster there wasn't any kid and there weren't any Fritos.

Instead, he was there, crouched against the wall, half a rat in his mouth. *Crunch* went the rat bones. *Crack-crunch*. I stared. He ate everything, even the tail, jerking the body into his mouth with little tosses of his head.

There wasn't a lot of blood and I never saw any guts or anything fall out of his mouth; in a way it was a lot more civilized than some of the kids tucking into a turkey burger on Cookout Night.

When he finished he looked at me, his skinny pink tongue flickering out to clean his whiskers. He was red, with those long black marks on his front legs that made him look like he was wearing evening gloves, and his eyes were a kind of yellow that almost glowed. I had never seen a fox up close.

Hi, I said.

His ears twitched.

Was it good?

He cocked his head. I squatted, plucking my shirt away from my stomach. We watched each other. He sat, tail curled against his side. I held out my hand, palm up. Neither of us moved. The woods behind us crackled and snapped, like cereal in milk, the sounds of nature doing its thing. At night you could hear something running out there—not the way we ran, with our feet dragging and our fat shaking all over the place, but something going fast. Trying to get away.

It's all right, I said. I won't hurt you.

He shivered.

Amber! one of the counselors yelled through the

doorway. I turned and the fox darted off, leaves spitting beneath his paws.

Shit, what! I yelled back. Wilson's head popped over the Dumpster.

What are you doing? she asked.

Taking a piss, I said.

Cool it with the language, jokester, Wilson said. We need you in the Circle.

Prayer Circle was time for us to sit on the floor in the rec room and hold hands and ask Jesus to make us skinny. We were supposed to say things like "I pray for the strength to run a mile Wednesday without stopping" or "I pray for forgiveness for eating outside my Calorie Plan." I thought about the fox, the way he ate that rat like it was nothing, so neat and easy. Looking at me afterward without any shame at all. It was my second week at camp and I weighed 192 pounds.

I didn't have to tell him to come, didn't have to tell him which room was mine; two days after I'd seen him by the Dumpster I was lying in bed when I saw his head slip beneath the window we had cracked open, the screen torn just enough for him to squeeze through.

It's you, I whispered. He stepped onto my shoulder, fur brushing my cheek. I sat up and made room for him on the pillow but he sat in my lap instead, a snack pie in his mouth.

For me? I whispered, and he dipped his head, laying the pie on my chest, eyes deep into mine, and I thought about how a person would never look at another person like that, for such a long time, hardly blinking. I tore the wrapper and slid the pie into my hand, breaking off a piece and offering it to him.

Do you like this? I asked, and he took the piece from me and we ate there in the near-dark, comfortable, like we'd done it a hundred times before. Our faces were so close I could almost count the hairs in his velveteen ears. The pie was cherry and the filling was thick, like glue, sticking to my teeth even after I swallowed.

When we were done he licked my lips. I jerked my head back; he paused, waiting, then did it again. His tongue was warm, smooth, clean; I opened my mouth and he got inside it like it was a jar of honey, like it was the best thing he ever tasted, his paws on my chest as if to hold me down as we licked each other clean.

This happened almost every night, night after night. He brought snack cakes, potato chips, red licorice, jerky. There was a convenience store a half mile down the road; in the woods there were garbage cans, summer cabins with kitchens, campers with coolers and picnic baskets. But I could only guess where he got what he brought, and every night it was something different.

What do I look like to you? I asked after our snack, feeling how I spread over the tiny bed like a bowl of spilled pudding.

Enormous, I said. Right? A blimp. I puffed out my cheeks.

He twitched that place above his mouth where the whiskers entered, two soft white lozenges I longed to touch but never did. *Don't*, his eyes said. He didn't like it when I said anything bad about myself.

It's just that I think you're so beautiful, I explained, but it was more than that; I had this weird ache when I looked at him, like his prettiness hurt me. He tucked his head beneath my hand, pressing it against my palm. I pet him. He kept butting his head against me, insistent, all four paws sinking into my stomach.

What? What do you want? I asked. Hm?

He rubbed his head back and forth in my hand.

More? Like this? I dug my fingers deep into his fur; he pushed hard against me. I was stroking him all over. He was so clean, so soft, almost meatless; I'd had cats heavier than him. He crouched between my breasts, back arching and slinking as I touched him, his tail tapping my thighs. I didn't think about what was happening. I just let it happen. I lifted my hips. He stretched his jaw to my chin, resting it there, his whiskers trem-

bling as he breathed his warm breath over my mouth.
Lauren snored above us. I swallowed a sigh and closed
my eyes.

I'd lost thirty pounds since the start of camp and I was
learning how to run without puking, how to lift weights
without feeling like I was going to pass out. I didn't have
to lie down to button my shorts. At mealtimes I told
everyone I wanted to be a vegetarian but in secret I was
still eating meat, hamburger patties and hot dogs he
got from someone's grill, studded with little holes from
where his teeth had split through the skin. I was eating
everything I had eaten before and more.

One night Wilson sat next to me at dinner all cozy
and said You know, God gave us animals to sustain us.
It isn't wrong to eat meat as long as we eat it in modera-
tion. She pointed her chin at the pile of chicken breasts
on the cafeteria counter. I said Yeah, I know, and chewed
a slice of cucumber dipped in nonfat ranch. Wilson
squeezed my wrist and told me that what she really
wanted to say was that she was proud of me, that I was
an example to the other campers, that she could see
Christ working in my life and that she hoped I could
see it, too. I swallowed the cucumber and smiled.

No matter how long I'd waited to see him, no matter
how much I wanted to do all the other things we did, the

food came first, and it always had to be slow. I loved that about him, how he took his time; nothing was rushed. He wanted to be with me. And though it was always him who decided everything, always him who made the rules, everything that happened felt right. We would eat, and then we talked a little, and then we'd go quiet, and then, when I thought it might not happen, that it would never happen again, his tail would start to swish across my thighs. He used his nose to catch the end of my T-shirt, pushing it up. His ears quivered beneath my palms. His chin rubbed against my breasts, his fur sliding all over me. I helped him get my underwear off my hips. His little teeth were like needles, sometimes nibbling at my skin, just so I would know they were there, that he could hurt me if he wanted to, could take a piece of me in his mouth and swallow it whole.

It was midnight when the dorm door was flung open and the light snapped on. He froze between my legs.

What the heck, Lauren murmured, creaking awake in the bed above me.

Room check, Wilson said, sweeping the room with a grim gaze I'd never seen; there were cookie crumbs on the floor, wrappers crammed beneath the pillow. I was propped up against the wall, my knees making a tent beneath the blanket.

You should be asleep, she said.

I was, I replied, gulping air. She strode toward me, her hand raised over the blanket.

Give it to me, she said.

I didn't move.

Give you what? I said.

Whatever you've got under there.

I could feel him panting between my thighs. I don't have anything, I said.

Amber, she warned.

I don't have my shorts on, I said.

I need you to make the right choice, she hissed.

No, I said. She snatched at the sheet; I snatched it back.

Get out of that bed, she said.

For chrissake, you can't get her in trouble for *masturbating*, Lauren said, loud. Wilson's hand flew back from the blanket. I flinched.

You girls—Wilson started. She swallowed, her hand to her chest, her face slack as if she had just been slapped. I stared at her without wanting to; she looked away.

You girls should be asleep, she finished.

Okay, I said, and she left.

I wasn't doing what you said I was doing, I said to Lauren in the dark, heat thick in my face.

I don't want to know what you're doing, she said.

She turned over and I thought about all her weight above me, straining the mattress, suffocating us.

I lifted the blanket so he could breathe. The moonlight from the window hit his eyes, turning them green. His nose quivered between my breasts, his fur slick with my sweat. His tail flicked against my legs again. *We can keep going*, he meant, but I shook my head. We waited. Finally I heard Lauren snore and I lifted my head to his; he took my bottom lip, very gently, between his teeth.

Good night, I whispered, and he slipped through the window, his tail bunching beneath the sill.

All during Circle Wilson kept giving me mournful little looks, her forehead puckered, like I'd hurt her feelings on purpose and she couldn't figure out why. I picked a piece of rubber from the sole of my shoe and rolled it between my fingers and when it was time for me to say something I just sat there like an idiot.

Amber? Wilson prompted, her knees poking from the hem of her shorts like two bony fists.

Pass, I said, pinching the ball of rubber between my fingers as hard as I could. There was a long pause. Ray sniffed. Marcie glanced at Lauren. Wilson cleared her throat.

Pass! I yelled.

———

After showers Lauren announced that there was going to be a "little party" in our room. I was sitting on my bed, combing my wet hair; she stood in front of me, hands on hips, her considerable midriff at eye level. Our dorm was the farthest from Wilson's room, and so the safest, sound-wise, to break rules in, or so she told me. Someone would find beers somewhere, someone else could maybe rustle up some snacks, we could relax.

Can't you do it outside or something? I protested. I don't want to get caught. We already got in trouble once.

We? she echoed, one pencil-thin brow arched as high as it could go. I wasn't allowed to pluck my eyebrows at home and I had the urge to touch one of them, to see if it was as thick as I suspected it was.

Fine, I said, and went on combing my hair, wondering how late they would stay, how long he would wait for them to leave.

It turned out they brought just one beer to share, along with a snack-size bag of chips. Also a roll of mints and a soggy napkin full of watermelon Jell-O cubes Ben had smuggled from dinner. Ray and Lauren sat on my bed; the rest of us sat on the floor. They were all, I guess, good-looking, aside from being fat; Marcie had a waist, Lauren had the best hair, and Ben was tall, the only one of us who walked without hunching over. Probably some other girls would be really happy to have been there, hanging out with what passed for Camp Covenant's popular crowd, but I just sat there sucking on a Jell-O cube, glancing at the window.

It smells weird in here, Marcie said, wrinkling her tiny nose.

Yeah, Ray said. They looked at me and I shrugged. It seemed like everyone was expecting Lauren to say or do something but she just stared, combing her hair back with her hand. It was hot with the window closed but no one made a move to open it and I realized that even though I had lost more weight than any of the girls I was still the biggest one in the room.

You want some? Ben asked, holding out the beer. I took a sip, wiping my lips on the back of my wrist, and handed the bottle to Lauren, who drained it in one long gulp before announcing a game of Spin the Bottle.

Three seconds, on the lips, she said.

What if it's girl-girl or guy-guy? Ben asked.

Same rules, Lauren replied. She spun first: the mouth of the bottle pointed at me, the butt at Ben. He smiled.

No, I said.

What do you mean, no? Lauren snapped, quick, like she'd been expecting me to resist.

We don't have to, Ben said.

Yes, you have to, Lauren insisted. Otherwise what's the point?

This is so childish, I said. Marcie rolled her eyes.

Like you're so mature. She was about to say something else but Lauren shot her a look and Marcie shut up. I stood and headed for the door.

Where are you going?

To the bathroom, I said.

You can't—

But I could and I did. I was barefoot and my hair was still damp and I knew they wouldn't come after me because they weren't my friends and they weren't really my enemies. They were just bored. I opened the back door.

There he was, on top of the Dumpster, sitting still. I took a step back, wiping my hands on the seat of my bike shorts. The tip of his tail rose and fell against the Dumpster lid.

You scared me, I said.

He cocked his head. Near his back foot was a marshmallow pie, mostly intact. With his nose he pushed it toward me: this was his way of saying *Here* or *Please* or *Eat*. Tonight I thought it meant *For you*.

We ate the pie in the light cast by the security lamp over the kitchen door; when we finished he licked his paws, then licked my hands.

Take me somewhere, I said.

He looked at me, his eyes almost all black. This was

a new look, one I couldn't read; I thought maybe he didn't understand.

Show me where you live, I clarified.

His fur rippled and his eyes got even darker. I touched the place behind his ear that was so sensitive; he turned his face into my palm.

Please. So we can be alone.

Again he just looked at me. The night was cooling, peppered with the sound of insects and leaves slipping against each other, the air with a smell of dirt so strong it was almost a taste.

Please, I said again. There was a rustle in the dorms; a head popped out of a window beyond the Dumpster—Lauren looking for me. He jumped down into the dirt and I ducked. Someone laughed, then was shushed. He put his paws on my knee and lifted his face to mine.

I closed my eyes, kneeling. His whiskers twitched in my hair, his nose against my ear. The woods were so close, and the camp seemed like a blight in the middle of it, along with Lauren and Ray and Marcie and Wilson and all the rest of them. And what was I? Something in between the camp and the woods, something between a blight and whatever the fox was. Beyond us I heard glass cracking and Lauren's harsh whisper, Ben's hysterical giggle.

Do you love me? I said, looking at the dirt, stirring my finger in it. He stopped my finger with his paw. I didn't want to look at him. I just looked down at my finger and his paw, the thinnest parts of us, trying to imagine a universe where they could be part of the same body.

I just want to go, I said, but we stayed right there.

He didn't come Monday night, or Tuesday; by midnight on Wednesday my stomach was the size of a walnut, shriveled and queasy. I tried to think: What eats foxes? How long do they live? How old was he? What diseases could he get? He could have been shot by some jerk with nothing better to do. He could be decaying in a pile of leaves or dragging a damaged limb through the underbrush, dying a slow dripping death, and I wouldn't know or be able to do anything about it.

I didn't sleep. Every sound sounded like him coming through the screen; the pillow against my cheek could have been his fur. The temperature dropped again and Lauren demanded we close the window; I told her no.

Why not? It's freezing, she complained.

I have asthma, I said. I can't breathe.

Bull, she said, but the window stayed open and he didn't come and I imagined the worst.

———

In the cafeteria the next morning everyone was going crazy over their rations of turkey bacon; the cook dropped some onto my plate, even though I didn't ask for it. I pushed my fork into the tough strips of flesh, expecting blood.

You need your protein, Wilson said, tapping me on the shoulder as she walked by. I pushed my tray away.

What's wrong? Lauren whispered, bending over her tray, and she seemed genuinely concerned. I closed my eyes, my arms crossed around my stomach. I could hear everyone chewing and swallowing and gulping and cutting and I wondered how I could have ever thought eating was a good idea.

I think she's sick, Lauren told Patton, and when he put his hand on my forehead I fainted.

I spent the day in the nurse's office. I ate half a chicken cutlet and sweet potato fries at dinner and Wilson smiled; when I got back to my room the window screen had been replaced and the sash was locked. I looked at Lauren and she shrugged. I stomped out and threw up everything into the toilet, pinning my hair to my chest with my arm.

We were running in the woods. A quarter mile from camp I saw him, tail high, slipping through some trees.

I stopped, the front of my shirt soaked through; a weird noise escaped my throat, a little cry or part of a word, a word that started out to be his name before I realized his name didn't exist.

He had something in his mouth: a sandwich, maybe one of the tuna fish triangles from yesterday's lunch. Whoever was on garbage duty must have dropped it, or else he'd found his way inside the kitchens and snagged it himself. The group was moving ahead, and I dropped to my knee, pretending to tie my shoe.

You okay? Patton called, looking over his shoulder. I nodded, waving to signal that I would catch up. I watched Patton's butt jump through the woods and then took off sideways into the brush, stepping fast through the trees where I'd seen him last.

He hadn't gone far; he was only a little ways from the path, circling a hole at the base of a rotting tree trunk, the sandwich in his mouth. Something snapped beneath my foot; he turned. Our eyes met.

He wasn't alone.

Clustered near the den was another fox, smaller and redder than him, and two kits, pressed against her side. Littered all around were candy wrappers and crusts and pits and cores: Food trash. Familiar trash. *My* trash.

What the fuck, I breathed. The kits reached their snouts to the sandwich; he dipped it to their mouths, not taking his eyes off mine as his kids nibbled the tuna fish from his lips.

I thought you were dead! I shouted, shaking. I was hot all over, my throat tight, like someone was stepping on it.

Who are they? I demanded, pointing at the others. Did you have them the whole time? Were you ever going to bother to even *tell* me?

He looked at me, so still except for the soft movement of his sides as he breathed. The other fox flicked her tail. The kits' eyes gleamed like glass beads. *Garbage garbage garbage* was all they heard when I opened my mouth. *Gobblegobblegobble.*

You're an asshole, I said, my palm sliding against a trunk, splitting away a tiny piece of skin. I picked up a twig and threw it. The other fox hissed; the kits curled behind her. He just stared.

Do something! I yelled.

He did nothing.

Crouching, I looked for a rock and I found one, a big one, sharp all over the top. Even with both hands I could barely lift it.

I ate deer meat once, I said, swallowing hard. I kicked a dog when I was ten. Don't think I can't do it. I can. I will.

What do you want from me, his eyes said. I dropped

the rock. He blinked. It was dinnertime and they would be looking for me and when they found me I would be in so much trouble.

I put out my hand. He came close. I dug my fists into his fur.

ACKNOWLEDGMENTS

Many, many thanks to my literary foxmother, Kathe Koja, whose work shaped my own so many years ago. You continue to set the bar. Thank you for lighting the way.

To fairy godfathers H. Peter Steeves and Matthew Specktor, whose faith opened doors, thank you.

To Meredith Kaffel and Emily Bell, the dream team, for all your guts and grace and wisdom. Thank you, thank you, thank you.

Thanks to all at FSG for making this book a book. To Joachim Brohm for spotting those cars on fire.

To my father, and the little one lost along the way, thank you for being.

To William and Charlotte, my good ones, you are my joy.

And to my twin, my muse, without whom these stories would and could never be—this is all, always, for you.